I Am the Law!

Mitchell Slade, a top US Marshal, is sent to clean up the New Mexico town of Hatfield. Within a few minutes of his arrival, four men lie dead under a shroud of smoke, and this sets the tone for Slade's stay.

It isn't long before the man who killed Slade's family, Brazos McGraw, shows up in town. The streets of Hatfield are ready to run red with blood unless Slade can stop his old enemy's reign of terror. And to do this will cost him much more than he is prepared to pay.

I Am the Law!

Hank J. Kirby

A Black Horse Western

ROBERT HALE · LONDON

ISBN 978-0-7198-1617-8

Robert Hale Limited
Clerkenwell House
Clerkenwell Green
London EC1R 0HT

www.halebooks.com

Typeset by
Derek Doyle & Associates, Shaw Heath
Printed and bound in Great Britain by
CPI Antony Rowe, Chippenham and Eastbourne

CHAPTER 1

ARRIVAL

Most folk who witnessed his arrival in Hatfield thought there was nothing special about the way he looked.

Somewhere between thirty and forty would be a fairly close guess at his age. The features were hard-bitten and had seen the rough side of life. His clothes were the usual range type and carried traces of the dust of a hundred-or-more different trails.

There was a well-used Colt in a weathered holster on his right side, and the butt of the Winchester rifle that showed above the saddle scabbard was scratched and chipped. The fact that the man still carried it after so long likely meant it shot well – *or mebbe the man shot well using that rifle. . . .*

It was there, anyway, and the horse he rode, a high-shouldered palomino, was also trail stained, but moved with long-stepping ease, answering the slight-est touch on the reins or heels, *pronto.*

These were things noted by the loungers on the porch of the saloon, drinking, telling and laughing at off-colour jokes and seeing who could outdo one another with tall tales.

They quietened as the rider stopped at the hitch-rail, swung down a little stiffly and tossed the reins' ends over the rail without tying ... which said a couple of more things about that trail-dusted horse, the way it set its feet and lowered its head in a relaxed, patient style. Waiting. . . .

The man slapped a cloud or two of dust from his clothes, nodded once to the watchers and went into the saloon through the weathered batwings.

Two minutes later, all hell broke loose.

There was a sudden roar of gunfire, one volley of five rapid shots standing out from the scattered crash of the other Colts. The loungers dived for cover as bullets from inside sent splinters flying across the porch; a window smashed musically. Then, just as suddenly as the sound had erupted, it ended, the echoes ringing in the ears of the loungers and passers-by who had frozen in mid-step at the first few shots.

They hadn't even had time to decide whether to dive for cover or run.

The new arrival appeared at the batwings, just closing the cylinder of the reloaded Colt, but not yet holstering it, and nodded amiably enough at the staring people.

Behind him, Cass Malone, the barkeep, appeared, his bar towel in both hands, his fat, ruddy face showing shock.

'J-Judas Priest! There – there's four dead men in there!' His wide eyes swivelled to the hard-faced rider who was standing by his horse now, tweaking one of its ears; it seemed to like it. 'He – he done it! Killed the sheriff an—'

'Christ!' breathed the closest lounger, moving back a few paces. He swallowed as the hard eyes of the stranger settled on him. 'What you wanna go an' do that for, mister?'

'He was trying to kill me.' The voice was deep and rough from a long, dusty trail.

All eyes swivelled to the barkeep, who nodded jerkily. 'S'right enough. Lew Towney took one look at him and went for his gun. Next thing, this feller's fanning his Colt's hammer and Lew goes down an' the three men with him.'

'They were trying to kill me, too,' the stranger said flatly and men who had crowded around the batwings inside the saloon murmured agreement.

'Well – who the hell are you?' asked a skinny man with a drooping moustache. 'I mean, you walk through the batwings – two minutes later we got four dead men piled up in the saloon! You couldn'ta been in town for more'n five minutes an' you're makin' the undertaker rich!'

The crowds that were gathering all looked at the stranger and he raked cool grey eyes around them and said, 'Name's Mitchell Slade. Deputy United States Marshal *I – am – the – law* whether you like it or not – and I'm here to stay, for a spell, anyways.'

There was lots of murmuring and blinking and staring. Someone said, 'Why the hell they send a US marshal to Hatfield? We're pretty much a law-abidin' town.'

There was quiet agreement, and a couple of very clear comments backing that statement. They were waiting for Slade's reply.

'Seems there's some as wouldn't agree with that. I'm here to sort things out.'

'Well, hell, killin' our sheriff is sure a great start!' a ragged voice said and it brought a few chuckles, but the marshal said calmly, 'He needed killing.'

'*What?*'

'*Who? Lew Towney?*'

'Hell, he was a good-enough sher'ff!'

'Yeah! He was OK to get along with for a lawman.'

'He kept a good town here! Now some gunslinger hidin' behind a law badge puts him six feet under Boot Hill.'

There were lots of similar comments hurled back and forth and Mitchell Slade listened to them all as he rolled a cigarette. He glanced up as he ran the tip of his tongue along the edge of the paper.

'All finished?'

There was something in the way he said it that made it clear they had *better* be finished, for he had something to say now. He fired up the smoke and exhaled.

'Your sheriff was corrupt.' He paused, letting the crowd have their say about that accusation and, when the angry comments died away, one by one he raked those grey eyes – now kind of chilled – around the townsfolk. 'Lew Towney was half-brother to Scuff McLean – I take it you know who he is?'

There was animated conversation and open shock showing on many faces at the marshal's statement.

'It's true,' Mitchell Slade said. 'I ain't about to spend an hour proving it to you, just take my word for it. He and Scuff had a deal going: Towney gave him the secret timetables and routes of the payroll deliveries, when the stageline was carrying a strong-box worth stealing, all that kind of thing. We're nor sure, but we think he was the one who tipped Scuff off about Wells Fargo bringing in that gold shipment from the diggings at Pembroke Springs. The driver *and* shotgun guard were killed in that hold-up . . and one passenger, another wounded. Helluva mess. But you know about that: it happened not seven miles from where we stand.'

That brought some instant comments and shock and consternation showed on many faces.

'Your sheriff was aiming to retire next year at age fifty! Not bad, eh? And he had himself a mighty fine nest-egg waiting for him – held by Scuff himself. . . .'

'Don't believe it!' shouted someone and several others echoed the words.

'You don't have to,' Slade told them flatly. 'We've been working undercover and we have all the proof we need, *and* that Towney was meeting a couple of Scuff McLean's men here today.'

'So they sent you in to – to kill 'em all!'

9

Slade looked at the thin-faced man with the heavy moustache who had spoken. 'I was sent to administer the law. It was Towney's decision to make a gunfight out of it.'

'You – you ain't no better'n a paid killer!' Blackie Norton, the town butcher, said, outraged. 'Judas! What kinda law is it sends a killer in to make an arrest?'

Slade waited until all the fuss and threats and general outrage had died down.

'I came to arrest Towney. Like I said, he chose to make a gunfight out of it. I b'lieve I've done my duty.'

'And the three others?'

'McLean's men, every one. We have all the proof required by law. We've prepared a lot of solid evidence and even set up lawyers ready for the trial – which, of course, won't need to take place now.'

'Nah! Dead men make lousy witnesses!' allowed a voice whose owner was lost in the crowd.

That got a good few laughs and Mitchell Slade even half-smiled.

'Cheaper, too,' he threw in. 'But you men got any complaints, you get 'em notarized by a proper attorney and I'll see they're passed along to the Chief Federal Marshal. I know I did the job I was paid to do.'

'Helluva lot of good that'll do poor old Lew Towney.'

'Well, it's up to you fellers. I told you: I am the law here until I wind up a few things and my report'll go in, then, too. You'll find everything's above board.'

10

Then suddenly there was a small commotion behind the front row of onlookers and Slade just caught a glimpse of a girl in town clothes – a sky-blue full-length dress with matching hat – and next thing his face was burning and his eyes were briefly rolling in their sockets as he ducked her second swing at him with her umbrella. He lifted an arm to parry the blow, grabbed her wrist and twisted roughly, bringing a small cry from her as she dropped her weapon, rising to her toes in an effort to ease the pain in her wrist.

The onlookers mostly just stared; a few swallowed uneasily. No one made a move to stop the big marshal, who shook his head, ears ringing, face tingling where she had struck him. 'Easy, ma'am, you're hitting a lawman.'

'You mean a *killer* and you're still able to talk, so I obviously haven't hit you hard enough!' she retorted, her voice high-pitched and breaking on the last word as she struggled to get free.

'Hard enough for me!' he admitted fervently. 'What the hell d'you think you're doing?'

She was unable to break his grip on her wrist. 'I'm . . . trying to get free so I can *kill* you!' He frowned as she added, very close to tears, 'Sheriff Towney was my father!'

He was silent for a few seconds. 'Well, if he was no better at fatherin' than he was keeping the law, you have to be better off.'

'Hey! That's pretty rough, Marshal!' the butcher yelled, and there were murmurings of agreement from the crowd.

Slade looked embarrassed. 'Sorry, miss. I didn't mean to upset you that way. I – well, I spoke outa turn.'

The girl's face was white, her dark eyes stark against the suddenly pale skin. There was a brief, horrified look as her eyes filled, one spilling tears that made a wet track down her high cheek. 'You – you cold-blooded *swine*!'

There was another low growl from the audience to make it obvious the majority agreed with the girl.

'Miss Towney, I'm right sorry you had to be here when it happened, but it's done and I have no regrets.'

'Hey! Ease up, Marshal!' roared the butcher, who took a step towards Slade, then stopped when he saw the man's face – *he didn't want to be added to the body-count.*

No one else wanted to stick their oar in apparently and the crowd began to shuffle restlessly.

'Someone better get the undertaker,' Marshal Slade suggested. 'I'll fix up all the legal papers with him.'

'Wait up,' said Hal Doone, the blacksmith. 'What you gonna do now? You said somethin' about us bein' "stuck with you for a while".'

Slade nodded. 'There're a few things from Towney's doings to clear up and that need legal support. I'll be around, doing the necesssary checking. Shouldn't take long unless he's got other gang members I dunno about. . . ?'

He waited for some sort of reply.

He didn't get one and he smiled crookedly.

'I am the law,' he said easily. 'But it don't – and won't – set easy with you folk, will it?'

'Will when you leave,' growled the butcher.

Marshal Slade's smile widened.

'That's what I figured. Just one thing, folks: I'll be quick as I can, but – don't get in my way.' He touched a hand to his hatbrim. 'Remember that and we'll get along fine.'

The girl who claimed to be the sheriff's daughter had been standing there, rigidly, aware of the drying tears on her now flushed cheeks – her hands opening and closing.

She glanced down and saw that he was standing on her damaged umbrella. Their gazes met and his face was hard and unbending. Her breathing was quickening as he saw by the rise and fall of her bosom and he tensed, ready for another attack.

'I'm still going to kill you!' she hissed.

'Woman killed a marshal in Sedalia, Missouri – aw, must be five years ago now – they hanged her.'

She stopped, stiffening. 'You lie!'

He shrugged. 'Contact the Federal Marshal's office, they'll confirm it.'

She frowned deeply, her full lips parted, and the tip of her tongue moistened them, as she cleared her throat and said, 'Even that would be worth risking.'

'Your choice, lady. I never shot a woman, but once. Well, there you are.'

His words stopped her and she glared at him,

looking a trifle confused, then hurried off abruptly, calling over her shoulder,

'*Murderer*!'

Mitchell Slade watched her cross the street with jerky strides, shoulders rigid, and slowly shook his head. Then he pushed past the barkeep and the others opened out to allow him to go back into the saloon.

'Let's get this mess in here cleaned up.'

CHAPTER 2

HAZARDS OF HATFIELD

'Look at my barroom!' complained the saloon owner, one Willard P. Johnson. 'Christ, bullet holes everywhere, splinters hangin' – an' I'm gonna have to replace that whole street-front window! Who the hell's payin' for all that?'

Marshal Mitchell Slade had set up a temporary office at a corner table in the rear of the saloon. Apart from Johnson's yelling, the big room was reasonably quiet now. Many of the drinkers who had scattered at the first gunfire had come back and they were all watching the big marshal, who now wore his official star badge on his shirt pocket.

He glanced up at the saloon man's whining complaints, didn't like the flickering restless eyes that never seemed to rest long enough to be read for expression, and flipped a handbill-sized printed form across the table. 'Fill that out, friend, and I'll see the Federal Office gets it.'

'And what'll they do with it? Stick it in a file and forget it?' Johnson lifted one corner of his mouth in a leer.

Slade shifted his gaze to the reddened face of the saloon man. '*Amigo*, I'd guess you're at an age where you oughta be watching your blood pressure more. Now why don't you just fill out that claim, and I'll start it through the normal process; might take a little time, but the repairs will be paid for.'

'You guarantee that?' snapped Johnson and actually took a step backward when he saw Slade's hardening face.

'You doubting my word? Close to calling me a liar if you are.'

Johnson blew out his cheeks, lifted his free hand quickly. 'N-now wait up! I – din' mean anythin' – but I've been in the saloon business a long time and—'

'I'd say if you aim to keep on in it, then just do what I told you and everything'll go faster and smoother. OK by you?'

'Sure! Sure, Marshal!' There was a sheen of sweat on the man's brow and the paper shook a little as he lifted it and folded it before putting it into one of his waistcoat pockets. 'I-I'll fill this out right away.'

Slade wasn't listening, didn't even look up from the papers on the table, started shuffling through them for the one he wanted.

He glanced across the big room to where a

swamper was mopping the floor and another washing down the bullet-pocked wall that had been splashed with blood. The bodies had already been efficiently removed by the town undertaker.

'Think I could do with a whiskey and a cold beer to wash it down,' the lawman said, and the saloon owner quickly flashed a smile.

'Sure, Marshal. Zeke, you heard.'

One of the barkeeps who had been watching and listening gave a small jerk and nodded, turning to the bottles behind his counter.

Mitchell Slade glanced up from his work when the drinks appeared, nodded his thanks and quickly tossed down the whiskey. He smacked his lips, grimaced a little at the liquor's bite, reached for the cold beer.

A couple of deep gulps went down easily and he sighed as he lowered the glass. 'Hits the spot, barkeep.'

Then he dived for the floor as a shotgun blasted and blew away half the table he had been sitting at, the papers erupting and flying about like a miniature snow storm.

He rolled across the floor, kicking the overturned chair aside, his Colt already in his right hand, the barrel searching for a target. He flicked the muzzle up slightly and triggered at the top of the piano across the room.

The fold-back lid split in long, sword-like splinters and the second bullet flung up a handful of the ivory keys as he leapt to his feet and launched himself across a neighbouring table. He kicked at the upright, now useless, piano. It rocked and slammed back almost to the wall, but it couldn't touch it because someone was crouched behind the piano and they cried out in fright.

A woman's startled scream.

Slade kicked another chair aside, reached into the space and dragged out the girl in the blue dress, which was torn in the process as she struggled in his hard grip.

She had dropped the shotgun – a single-barrelled 12-gauge Greener, his experienced gaze told him – and he hauled her up roughly, pushing her back against the wall, while waving his Colt in front of her face.

'You damn fool, woman! Never even had enough sense to use a double barrel in case you missed!' He shook her and she whimpered in awful frustration and maybe a touch of fear, for this Slade was a frightening man, especially when riled. Her blue hat had long gone, but the blue dress was the same except for several fresh rents in the fabric. A few strands of her dark hair clung to her face. 'I could throw you in the Women's Prison till you're old and grey for what you just did! Dammit! I'll tell you just once more: your father was trying to shoot me in the back when I spotted him in a corner of the bar mirror so I drew on him. Now that's it! You come at me one more time, with a shotgun, knife or even a broken coffee cup, and I tell you true: *I'll shoot you where you stand*!'

Nobody who heard that threat doubted that he

meant it . . . certainly not the girl.

She sobbed once and he caught her with an arm about her slim waist as her legs gave way. He jerked his head at one of the saloon men and the man hurriedly skidded a chair across. Mitchell Slade slammed her down into it unceremoniously.

'Stay there and shut up! Better still, when your legs are working again, get the hell outa here – and remember what I said, because I'm not in the habit of making idle threats.'

She gulped and her chest heaved as she fought for breath, emotion choking her. Willard Johnson signalled irritably at a bunch of saloon girls who had been watching and two of them hurried across, took the girl's unresisting arms and led her away.

'Give her a brandy and see her home – right to the door, mind!' snapped Johnson.

He watched them leave and turned back to the lawman.

'I'll be claiming on what you done to my piano, too! Hell, I only brought it in from Santa Fe a couple of months ago.'

'Try your luck,' Slade said, uninterestedly. 'Look! You worry about your damn saloon, but you take time to gimme a list of names of the men that sheriff hung out with – *No*! Goddammit, never mind stalling! I want that list now, or you'll be making a claim for fire damage, too! On a pile of ashes that used to be your saloon.'

'Jesus! What kinda damn lawman are you! You're actin' more like one of Lew Towney's hardcases!'

19

'Gimme the hardcases' names!' Slade said bleakly, and Johnson fumbled out a kerchief and mopped at his face.

'Sure! Sure, take it easy, Marshal. I'm upset about my saloon – but, I'll give you what you need—'

'Write 'em down – and quickly. And get someone to watch out for that crazy damn woman. I've got enough to handle without worrying about getting a load of buckshot or a bullet in the back.'

Willard Johnson kept nodding. 'Sure! Sure! Whatever you say, Marshal, whatever you say.'

'I say – *get a damn move on!*'

He learned her name was Margarita Chavez.

'What happened to "Towney"?' Slade asked Johnson.

'Aw, she married some Mex freighter against her father's wishes. He got killed, supposedly helpin' Lew Towney on some project he had goin' accidental-like.'

'*Supposedly* helping out the sheriff?'

Willard Johnson looked uncomfortable and shrugged. 'Well, Lew kinda ran things to his own likin' when he was sheriff – an' the fact was, he *didn't* like Ricardo Chavez, his son-in-law, said he didn't want no grandkids of his carryin' any greaser blood or name.'

Slade frowned. 'Sounds like it wasn't exactly a marriage made in Heaven as far as Towney was concerned.'

Johnson smiled crookedly. 'The Other Place'd be

20

closer. . . . Anyways, that's what happened to Chavez.'

'How did the girl take it?'

Johnson blew out his cheeks. 'Half-sister to a goddamn hurricane! I dunno whether she really loved this Chavez – most folk said she married him just to spite old Lew – but she told Lew she wasn't droppin' her married name and would have it printed on all her belongings and use it wherever she went – and if he din' like it, he could lump it.'

Slade looked more puzzled than ever. 'Sounds like she hated Towney's guts. Yet she's trying to kill me for shootin' him.'

The saloon man shrugged. 'She's got a temper. See, Lew married a good-looker but he din' treat her right and she run out on him with a *Mex*, and – well, that's why he don't – didn't – like greasers. He figured he'd been made a fool of, you know, and. . . . Well, any Mexes were a long way down Lew's popularity lists.'

Slade shook his head slowly. 'I'm sure glad I never got hitched! Is she crazy, or what? I mean, seems like she must've hated Lew Towney, yet she's after me because I killed him in self-defence. That sounds crazy to me.'

'Be her mother's fiery streak – and she had a beaut! Aw, I guess Margarita is pretty fiery herself an' – well, I can't explain it, but I'll say this: it don't surprise me that she's tryin' to kill you and I bet it don't surprise anyone else in Hatfield, neither. Just . . . just the kinda thing you'd expect from her. And she *will* make her try, Marshal. Take that as gospel.'

21

Slade was silent briefly, then grunted. 'Don't sound so damn happy about it. Looks like I'll soon have to be claiming I've shot *two* women.'

'Judas! You – you'd really shoot her?'

'Well, I wouldn't stand still and let her shoot *me*!'

'N-no. I-I s'pose not. Judas Priest, but I'm glad I ain't you, Slade!'

'Stop gloating! Or hoping! It might never happen.'

Willard Johnson smiled slyly. 'Wanna bet. . . ?'

Just on sundown, Mitchell Slade left his table in the saloon and crossed the dusty street to a diner he had noticed, and where a man was now lighting lanterns and hanging them from the entrance awning.

The man, short, grey-haired, started slightly when he saw the lawman, burnt his finger on the vesta he was using and shook his hand wildly.

'Er – evenin', Marshal. Go right on in. Wife's got beefsteak stew on tonight and the best apple pie this side of Santa Fe. Order what you like, it's on the house.'

Slade paused and looked up at the man on the ladder. 'I see your name on the window says you're Seamus O'Malley.'

'Yessir. And right proud of it.'

'German, is it?'

'Hell, no! It's about as Ir— Aw, you're joshin' me!'

'Kind of. Like I'm hoping *you* were joshing trying to bribe me.'

O'Malley almost fell off the ladder. His mouth

worked without sound for a few seconds. 'I – uh – hell, I wasn't trying to *bribe* you. Just bein' friendly.'

'Uh-huh. Well, while I'm off duty, which includes mealtimes, I'm just an ordinary citizen, O'Malley. And I pay my way. Thanks for the offer but that's the way it is.'

O'Malley was sweating now and wiped some that had gathered at his eyebrows with a colourful kerchief, nodding several times. 'S-sure – er – I understand. Sorry, Marshal, I din' mean—'

'So you already said. I'll let you know what I think of your wife's cooking.'

He ducked past the ladder and entered and O'Malley blew out his cheeks, frowning. '*No one's that blamed honest!*' he murmured to himself.

Slade enjoyed the meal and had O'Malley call his wife out where he told her she was a fine cook, left the exact money beside the plate and went out into the evening that had darkened the Hatfield streets.

He sat on a bench outside the general store, rolled and smoked a cigarette, and when it was finished went into the store and bought some cheroots and a box of strike-anywhere vestas. He strolled casually through the town, looking in on businesses that were still trading, startled a young couple having a kiss and a cuddle in the darkened doorway of a bootmaker's shop, and paused outside the saloon. He decided he didn't want another drink and went to the rooming-house where he had booked a room. As the clerk at the reception desk handed him his keys, his hand was shaking. Slade looked him squarely in the eyes.

'Something wrong?' When the man hurriedly shook his head, he asked, 'You ailing for something?'

'N-no, sir. 'I-I'm fine.'

Slade's gaze didn't waver. 'I'll believe you, friend, but a thousand wouldn't. I get any messages while I was out? No? Any enquiries? Like, which room is mine, or. . . ?'

The man was drenched in sweat and he dropped his gaze, tried to get his hands out of sight under the counter. The clerk cleared his throat, spoke in a hoarse whisper. 'You could use the outside stairway if you wanted. Your room has a curtained window that looks out above them stairs. Tall feller like you might even be able to see into the room – just over the edge of the sill, you know? I mean, if you wanted to check or – anythin'. . . .'

Slade nodded. 'Friend, I think you might be ailing for something that could be dangerous to your health. Why don't you take the night off? I can find my own way to my room.'

The man's tongue flickered around his dry lips and he started gathering his things as the marshal moved across the foyer towards the rear door that led to the outside stairway.

He went up quietly, key in his left hand, Colt in his right. He pushed back his hat and let it hang down his back by the thong as he crouched under the window in the wall almost at the top of the stairs. Pressing against the wall he lifted his head slowly, very slowly, until his eyes were just past level with the sill – and he could see beneath the bottom of the cheap curtains.

The room was too dark to see anything. But he waited, straining to hear, cursing the night sounds of Hatfield's streets and the residents who were using them.

He had to admit that he couldn't say if anyone was in his room or not, so carefully opened the door at the top of the stairs and stepped into the badly lit passage. *There was a quick movement in the shadows just past his room door – like a man trying to flatten himself against the wall.*

Mitchell Slade straightened his shoulders and stepped out into the passage, closing the door behind him with a slight thud, rubbing hands together as if from the cold – there was only a slight nip in the air so he hoped he hadn't overdone things.

Then he moved up to the door, fumbling his key into the lock, and suddenly lunged for the shadows where he had glimpsed the waiting man. There was a loud gusting as the man was slammed back against the wall, breath driven from him. But he tried to bring up the six-gun he held. Slade grabbed the wrist, twisted brutally and the man yelled, his legs buckling at the pain as tendons tore and his fingers were crushed against the gun.

Slade used a shoulder under the man's chin to pin him against the wall.

'How many are in there?' gritted the marshal and the man sobbed a curse. Slade lifted a knee into his groin, hard enough to make him gag. 'How . . . many?'

'None, eh? Well, sorry I was so rough, friend. Let's go in and have a drink to square things up, eh. . . ?'

'*No!*' The man made the short word into a choking sound, alive with fear, as Slade dragged him in front of the door, planted a boot against his buttocks and straightened his leg violently.

' The man started to scream as his body smashed open the door and then the night was full of a roaring explosion and the broken body hurtled back into Slade and knocked him floundering, even as instinctively he lifted arms to protect his face from whistling buckshot and flying splinters.

CHAPTER 3

'TO HELL WITH THE LAW!'

'I think he's dead, going by all that blood,' opined Jacob Dern, the town undertaker, who had come speedily and unerringly to the place of tragedy, looking for new 'customers'.

Doc Garner glanced up from where he knelt on the landing at the head of the rear stairway of the rooming-house – careful he didn't get any of the blood or gore on his trousers.

'Jacob, you're too impatient – oh, you'll have one "customer" when you've . . . gathered . . . him up, but the marshal is merely unconscious – in fact, beginning to stir – and ninety per cent of the blood drenching him belongs to the unfortunate who opened the door.'

'Looks like he crashed it open to me, Doc,'

allowed one of the onlookers crowding in. 'Maybe the marshal threw him at it, sort of. . . ?'

That caused a murmur and the medico frowned, manoeuvred a little so he could let Mitchell Slade rest his head on his bent leg. 'That might be a little more comfortable, Marshal. I'm afraid your head is going to ache badly: you were very close to the explosion, shielded by – whoever – led you here.'

Slade frowned and made a couple of guttural sounds before his eyes opened and he looked around, obviously taking in the situation as full consciousness slowly returned.

'What was it? Dynamite?' His voice was raspy and the words a little blurred but he cleared his throat as a man in clothes stained with leather dye held a glass of water to his lips. He sipped gratefully.

'Was a double-barrel, sawed-off Greener, Marshal. Set up on the end of the bed, just far enough inside to let the door fully open.' He gestured briefly to the bloody bundle on the floor beside the kneeling sawbones. 'Old Chuck took the full blast – right, Doc?'

'I'm reasonably certain so.' The medico was working over the marshal, cutting away his left shirt sleeve and then ripping the cloth down to reveal the lawman's white chest – now peppered with bruised and bleeding holes from some of the the buckshot. 'You're a lucky man, Marshal. If you'd walked into that blast, we'd've been collecting you in a sack.'

He helped Slade struggle to a sitting position and leaned him back against the wall.

'Chuck Riddel going in first took the full force of

28

it and, well, gave you sufficient protection to survive. . . .' The doctor's comment was gently probing. He arched his eyebrows slightly as Slade looked at him sharply, accepted the blood-spattered cloth offered, and wiped his face over.

'He was kinda reluctant. Had to persuade him a little. I reckon he knew what was waiting.'

'Someone doesn't like you very much, Marshal.'

'Used to that, but I've got me an idea who it was.'

'Well, I'm glad I'm not the one you suspect.'

'Makes you lucky, Doc.'

The crowd had all been talking or whispering, but Slade's words silenced them abruptly. The doctor frowned.

'Well, I'll gladly leave that part to you. . . . I've washed and covered the two deepest gouges. The rest I've dabbed with the world's favourite antiseptic . . . iodine. Nothing too serious, but you'd benefit from a day or so's rest and not using that left arm any more than necessary. In fact, a sling would be beneficial.'

'Obliged, Doc. Just glad it's not my gun arm you want to tie up. No sling, Doc. I've had worse than this on the training course.'

He struggled to get to his feet and the medic and a townsman helped him up. He swayed a little, put out his right hand to steady himself against the wall and slowly raked his gaze around at the gawkers.

'Lookin' for someone special, Marshal?' asked the sawbones.

'Thought I saw the Chavez woman on this side of

the street when I was crossing—'

'Margarita! Good Lord, you don't suspect—?'

'She did try once before to shoot me.' Slade noticed one townsman who seemed eager to speak. 'You see her, too, friend?'

'Well, I never seen her then, but she was over this way earlier and, then, of course, after the gun went off an' half the town showed up, I dunno where she went, but she left just as you were comin' round. You might find her at home.'

'Where's that?'

The man frowned, reluctant now, sorry he had said so much, maybe. 'Aw, she's got a little house out along Cannon Street, was her father's. Only five houses in the street an' hers is the middle one. Could take the time to show you, if you want. . . ?'

'Thanks anyway, I'll find her if I need her. She might've seen something helpful.'

Several people turned to look at each other, some with raised eyebrows, others with frowns.

Whether he had meant to or not, Marshal Mitchell Slade had made it fairly clear that he definitely *would* want to talk to Margarita Chavez.

Despite the doctor's admonition about resting he left the area, gently holding his left arm with his right hand so it didn't swing so much with his movements. He didn't particularly like doing it, because it put his right hand further away from his six-gun.

Not that he thought whoever had rigged the death trap would try again so soon, but. . . .

He bought a new shirt at the general store and put

30

it on out back of the shop, then went to see the rooming-house owner, a man named McKendrick.

He was middle-aged and had the pseudo tough look of a man who dealt with all types of people who wanted to rent one of his rooms. He was courteous enough to Slade but didn't seem very happy to see the lawman and only opened the door to his living quarters after Slade had threatened to kick it in.

'You left the scene of a crime on property that you own, mister. In my book, that needs an explanation. What say you. . . ?'

'Wasn't anythin' I could do there, Marshal,' McKendrick answered evenly. 'I can't tell you anything. What's wrong?'

He straightened as he looked at Slade's attitude: the lawman was staring at him hard.

'I know you, don't I?'

'Sure you do, I rented you the room.'

'*Before that!*' the marshal said crisply. 'Yeah, you had a moustache and a beard, one of them pointed little things. Take off your hat.'

'Aw, listen—' The man jumped when Slade reached out and swept the hat off – and McKendrick instinctively and swiftly put his hands up to his curly, grey-streaked hair. 'OK – I'm bald. This is a wig. Cost plenty, too, from a theatre company that—'

He let his shoulders slump as Slade said, 'McKendrick – bend it a mite and you can get Rick Kenny. Right?'

McKendrick shrugged and nodded, half-smiling. 'Just figured a change of name mightn't hurt.'

31

'Uh-huh. Green River, Wyoming – what? Two – three years back?'

'Two-and-a-half. I-I'm still grateful you took that local posse off my back: never quite savvied why you let me go but— You need any help now, you only gotta ask.'

'I let you go, Mac, because I recognized someone in that so-called posse – even without his pointy li'l beard like yours. His face had dried blood an' small cuts from him shaving quickly to get rid of it. Admitted later he framed you 'cause you could easi-ly've been mistook for him, so, if he got rid of his own beard and pointed you out to the others. . . . It was a rough description but good enough to nearly get you lynched for that robbery. He's still in jail.'

'Was hopin' I'd come across you sometime to thank you. I just quit that town and kept goin', ended up here.'

'Good to see you're prospering.'

'Wouldn't say that. Oh, I'm livin' OK, got me a wife, do some horse-tradin' an' got this roomin'-house, but I ain't rich. And my offer to help you – anytime – still stands.'

'Fine. You know what I'm after.'

McKendrick looked a little uncomfortable. ' 'Bout all I can tell you is it was the only room I had vacant. We're prettyin'-up the others an' the one you hired was the only one finished that didn't stink of paint.'

'Go on.'

'That's it. I can't tell you if anyone went into the room after you booked it an' the wife turned down the bed and so on.'

'What about Chuck Riddel?'

'Chuck? He rents a room here – comes an' goes.'

He was looking quizzically at the lawman and Slade said, 'They hanged his brother for murder and robbery down in El Paso, coupla months back, on my evidence.'

'Judas! You think he. . . ?'

'Good chance of it, I reckon. Margarita Chavez was here earlier, too. Saw her coming out of your foyer.'

McKendrick frowned. 'You're not thinkin'—! Aw, no! She an' the wife like cookin' and often swap recipes. She left one for Ellie at the counter here. Aw, shoot! I've forgot to pass it on yet! They want it for some Ladies' Club party that's comin' up.' He started patting his pockets, then paused when he saw the marshal's impatience.

'Oh, yeah, now I recollect! Margarita dropped it and it fell on my side of the counter and I had to get down and pick it up – an' I put it . . . now *where* did I put the damn thing? Hell, if I don't give it to Ellie in time, she'll stick me in the oven. Hey, Marshal!'

But he was talking to empty space: he could see the lawman through his front window striding down the street.

'Wonder what his hurry is?'

The Chavez woman answered his hard rap on her door almost at once and Slade figured she had watched him come down Cannon Street straight to her house.

She was wearing an apron over a white blouse and a striped skirt, a trace of flour on her hands and a smudge just above her left eye where she had no doubt brushed her hair aside.

'What do you want? I heard you'd been shot or something.'

'Don't sound so disappointed – I'm still able to get around. Can I come in?'

'No.'

He saw her unfriendly gaze move to the edge of the bandage showing where his shirt was unbuttoned.

'You'll be pleased to know some of your buckshot got past Chuck Riddel . . . and it hurts . . . but it's not fatal.'

She stiffened, features tightening with rising anger. '*I don't know any "Chuck Riddel"!* And *my* buckshot! You're accusing me of setting up that shotgun in your room?'

'It was a double-barrelled one. Thought you might've taken my earlier advice about that.'

The closing door almost broke his foot when he thrust it forward to jam it. Pain shot up his leg. His hands gripped the quivering door edge as she strained to close it, throwing her weight into it now.

'Don't be stupid, woman! he gritted. 'I could ram my shoulder into this hard enough to knock you clear across the room. Let me in.'

'I-I could claim forced entry!'

He grunted. 'You'd have to explain why you were trying to stop a US Marshal from doing his duty. Dunno of a judge anywhere in the country who'd find in your favour.'

She held out for a few heartbeats longer, then stepped back suddenly, hoping the abrupt lack of resistance would bring him stumbling into the house.

But Slade was an old hand at such tactics, held the door, then slammed it against the wall. She jumped back swiftly with a cry of alarm, but rage soon coloured her face as he came in and kicked the door closed behind him.

She turned and ran down a short passage, the lawman striding quickly after her, into a small kitchen: he smelled a cake cooking but doubted he would be offered a piece.

Then she spun to face him, holding a long-bladed carving knife. 'Don't touch me!' she gritted.

'Lady, if I had my gun in my hand I wouldn't even try!' He lifted his hands away from his side, wincing as pain spread through his wounds.

'Oh! You are hurt after all!' she said brightly. 'Seriously, I hope. A possible – amputation, perhaps?'

'No – and it's not even my gun arm, so I can still shoot.'

'Like you shot my father!'

'Look! You know the story on that, I'm sorry it's upset you, and I can savvy how it would, but it's done! It was him or me, and you know my preferences.'

35

'You are a cold-blooded swine, aren't you!'

'Setting up that shotgun in my room was pretty cold-blooded, too.'

She blinked. 'That's what you think I did?'

'Why wouldn't I? You'd already tried to shoot me . . . and you "managed" to drop that recipe you were handing McKendrick in his foyer. It'd be an easy job to reach across the counter while he was picking it up and take down the key to room number nine – the one I'd rented.'

She stared belligerently, but, slowly, the knife was lowered – not all the way, but at least to waist level. 'You must have a very low opinion of me. All right, I admit I wanted to kill you. I was a little crazy, I suppose, for a while—' She suddenly stamped her foot. 'Oh! Damn you! Why am I telling you this!'

'I'm always interested in what motivates people – specially if they're trying to kill me.'

There were tears in her eyes now but he did not relax: he knew there was a storm of emotions wrenching at her. She looked at him coldly. 'I *will* avenge my father!' Her voice was little more than a whisper.

'Lady, you are one stubborn woman! But I haven't changed my mind, either: try to kill me and I'll shoot you, even if it's the last shot I ever make.'

She gasped, staring: *somehow she knew he meant that.*

CHAPTER 4

MORE GUNS

It seemed to many of the Hatfield residents that Mitchell Slade was plumb loco.

All because he took a room in the saloon – top floor, centre, yards from the two stairways, one of which led up from the bar, the other for guests who wanted to reach their rooms without first having to thread their way through noisy drinkers in the bar proper, or dodge the sick and staggering who were looking for the lavatory area or any way out into one of the back alleys.

'Lot of people movin' about and lots of noise over there,' warned McKendrick, as Slade packed his gear in the room where he had spent the night.

'That's OK. But it's near the showgals' dressing rooms and they've got watchers crawling all over the place. You try to get into the area without they recognize you, or don't show your room receipt when

37

they ask for it, and you'll find yourself hunting up a quiet corner of the stables to sleep in, or wake up in the alley with a sore head and maybe some busted ribs and the cats lookin' at you ... looking down at you, that is.'

McKendrick pursed his lips. 'Yeah. Have heard of that happenin'. I got no special axe to grind, Marshal, but I do have a couple – well, kinda hard men who either can't find ordinary jobs, or don't want to, and they're willin' to sorta work part-time for me. Like now and again I have special *friends* passin' through and just to make sure they don't get hassled, my boys look after 'em.'

'Till it's safe for 'em to leave, right?'

McKendrick's tongue poked at one of his cheeks. 'Yeah, that kinda thing. You seem to savvy what I mean, and – qualify, if you'd like to hire a couple of these boys?'

'I might forget they're s'posed to be looking after me and throw 'em in jail.'

McKendrick looked genuinely shocked. 'Judas, man! I'm offering to give you a couple bodyguards! An' you're talkin' *jail*! Sure, you'd know their backgrounds, but only cost to you'd be to look the other way sometime – if it'd help 'em out. Sound all right?'

The marshal smiled thinly, the first time McKendrick – or possibly anyone else in Hatfield – had seen even that much of a smile on his hard face.

'Mac, I think your heart's in the right place for you.'

'Aw, I wouldn't get anythin' out of it. Just so long

as I knew you were safe, you know? Aw, sometime I might kinda have to – *remind* you – how I took care of you when you stayed in our town, but that's fair enough, ain't it?'

Slade slapped the man across the shoulders and McKendrick staggered, fighting for balance.

'Mac, that's what would worry me. You'd always be there to *remind* me.'

'But that's life, ain't it? I mean, you scratch my back, an' I'll scratch yours. Everybody's happy.'

Slade was shaking his head slowly before the other had stopped speaking, spreading his arms in mid-action.

'Not everybody, Mac. Thanks for the thought, but I'll pass.'

McKendrick couldn't hide his disappointment but he was a realist: it had been worth a try. And he knew Slade was a man to ride the river with, and if, at some future time, he *did* find a chance to repay a favour, then he would, even if it'd only been offered but not accepted.

'I run a good line in hosses if ever you need some for, say, a posse?'

'Not just yet, but tell you what,' Slade said suddenly, interrupting McKendrick's thoughts and lifting his hopes – briefly and disappointingly. 'There's a couple of fellers slouching around your place who looked kinda familiar. Wanted dodgers are always a mite blurred, you know, so I'm not *quite* sure. They *could* be fugitives: nothin' too serious or I wouldn't be talking now, I'd be throwing 'em in the local jail. You know who I mean? A long, redheaded streak of misery, and his pard not much bigger'n a schoolkid. . . .'

McKendrick cleared his throat: he had gone a couple of shades paler. Then he snapped his fingers.

'Oh, hell, I know the men you mean! Red Connor an' I think they call the other one – the shorty – "Big" Jock, some name like that. Funny, when they came to me with a note from a friend of mine down in Las Cruces, I had an inklin' I might've seen 'em someplace – or their pictures. I was wonderin' what to do about 'em. I owe this friend a lot, see, and don't want to let him down.'

'I'll be rising early, Mac, real early. Tell 'em not to make too much noise when they quit town.'

'Yeah, yeah, OK.' McKendrick dabbed at sweat on his face now with a kerchief too small for the job. 'I-I'm glad you – you're playin' straight about this, Mitch.'

'Always try to play it that way, Mac. Had an itch between my shoulders – figured you might have one, too. You know – *scratchy-scratchy*. . . ?'

McKendrick looked kind of sickly and nodded vigorously. 'I'll go find 'em. Think I know where they hang out.'

'Figured you might. . . . If there's any trouble, you know where to find me.'

'Er, matter of fact, I don't. Where you headed?'

'Just around town. Maybe looking for the next step along in the "Shuffle" or sometimes called the "Pipeline". Ain't that your second business: slipping

40

a man in a hurry on to some wagon-train headed for hell-knows-where, putting 'em in touch with someone who can lead 'em into wild country where they can hide out in safety? Guess that could be profitable – but dangerous, too.'

McKendrick's jaw was sagging now. 'How – how the hell you know so damn much? You only just arrived in town!'

Slade treated him to one of those rare smiles.

'They give us homework to do in the Marshals' Service, Mac, just like school. You know what's good for you, you take time to do it otherwise it could be your last assignment in more ways than one. Me, I've always enjoyed reading – keeps you abreast, even *ahead*, of the times.'

McKendrick nodded miserably. 'I'm – learnin'.'

'Knew you were smart, Mac. Just make sure those fellers we been talkin' about are smart enough to get my message: they better not still be in town by sun-up.'

'They won't be happy.'

'Aw, gee, now, I wouldn't want to upset 'em.'

'Er – well, I dunno, but— Yeah, sure. OK. I'll see they move on – you got my word.'

Slade smiled faintly. 'Good of you to give it, Mac, worthless though it may be. Here, you can borrow my kerchief to wipe the sweat off your face, then go tell Connor and the other feller *they're leaving town!*'

It wasn't quite as easy as that.

McKendrick told his clients, all right, and there

41

was a deal of cursing, and Red Connor drove one fist into the palm of of his other hand.

'Goddamn marshal! Who the hell's he think he is? I mean, we're only waitin' for you to fix the time for us to go. Why the hell'd he want to get bossy?'

'Because he's a goddamn lawman, that's why.' The small man's voice was surprisingly deep for the size of his chest, and those pinched-down green eyes looked – frightening, seems the best word. Look into those mean little eyes and you don't even think about the size of their owner.

They were pure killer's eyes – under certain circumstances, of course – and these circumstances seemed to be just *right* now and McKendrick felt his heart give a lurch.

'Hold it, Jock. Judas Priest, don't even think of takin' on *this* marshal. You heard what he done in a couple of minutes of hittin' town? I mean, Lew was no slouch with a gun, nor was his so-called deputies, Handy, 'n' Milo, but they never stood a chance. I seen it: five *fanned* shots and four dead men on the floor!' He snapped his fingers. 'Quick as that.' Then shook his head slowly. 'No, sir, leave like he wants. There'll be other times we can do business.'

'What if we don't wanna leave?' asked Red.

McKendrick threw up his hands. 'Then *don't*, for Chris'sakes! But just go get yourself killed somewheres away from my place so *I* don't have to fight him!'

The two wanted men both gave McKendrick a hard stare and then looked at each other.

'What you think, Jock?'

'I think mebbe this marshal is gonna be a big pain in the butt.'

'Yeah, well, in that case I guess I've got more pain than you.' Red turned his head a little and winked at McKendrick so the small man couldn't see.

Big Jock's face hardened – it could have been comical but there was something in those deadly eyes that reached out and made Red Connor mighty uneasy for being so stupid as to make fun of Jock's size.

'I mean – I-I'll make a bigger – target . . . er . . . but you still got more advantage than me, or even Mac here.'

McKendrick swiftly shook his head: he had no intention of getting involved in this silliness which could turn right ugly, as he'd seen on a couple of other occasions.

'That means . . . what?' Jock demanded quietly.

'Well, you got more chance of dodgin' bullets than someone . . . er . . . like me.' Red finished lamely, realizing he had painted himself into a corner. 'They'll likely go right over your head, an' – an'—'

'Because I'm so *short*!'

'Uh, I din' mean to rile you, Jock. . . .' Connor tried a crooked smile now but could see it wasn't going to work. 'Aw, I just thought there was a funny side to it.'

'Well, lemme tell *you*, my height is just right for plantin' my shots in the *belly* of long streaks of misery about your size!' He cupped one hand behind an ear.

'Huh? Don't hear you laffin!'

McKendrick forced a short laugh. 'Hey, Jock, that's a good one! I sure hope you can line up on Slade's gut.'

'Just what I figure to do,' Big Jock said flatly, with a surprisingly murderous look on his dinner-plate-sized face.

'Aah, *hell*!' said Connor and, with a resigned sigh and tightening of his mouth, took out his six-gun and began to check the loads. He glanced across at the now worried McKendrick. 'Relax, Mac, we're goin' all right, but it won't be quietly. Not now that Jock's got his dander up!'

'Thanks to you, damn your hide, Red! Just don't expect no back-up from me! Not agin Mitchell Slade!'

'Then you ain't no more use to us!' snapped Big Jock, as he rammed his six-gun deep into McKendrick's ribs and cocked the hammer.

McKendrick gave a muffled cry of alarm, face draining of blood. His voice was shaky, as he jumped back against the wall several paces away. He slithered down a little, lifting his arms across his face.

'Hell, Jock! Easy, man! We're friends, ain't we. . . ?'

Jock looked up at the staring Connor. 'You figure he's a real friend, Red? I mean, everythin' he does for us costs us a fistful of dollars.'

'Aw, well, that's just business, Jock!' the sweating McKendrick said hastily. 'Everythin' else from here on in is free for you fellers. OK? Not a dime more to pay.'

'Mighty generous of you, Mac,' said Red.

'Yeah,' said Big Jock. 'Real generous. But we'll leave town, just like this damn Slade wants' – he paused – 'which don't, of course, mean we mightn't come back when we want. Sound all right to you, Red?'

Connor grinned, watching McKendrick squirm.

'*Damned* all right, Jock! *Damned* all right!'

'Listen,' McKendrick said with an urgent tone. 'Don't even *think* of killin' Slade, now or later! A murdered marshal and they'll send in a whole troop of 'em, or even the goddamn army. An' none of us'll make a dime. Or even if we made a dollar or two, we wouldn't live to enjoy it! Now, I'm serious, fellers, *don't try to kill Slade!*'

Red and Big Jock looked at each other.

There was a whole lot more than disappointment on their faces.

Angry as they were, they knew McKendrick spoke gospel.

A dead federal marshal could mean the end of the world for whoever made him that way.

But. . . .

There was *always* a 'but' – that was life.

CHAPTER 5

NIGHTWALK

The word had gotten around: Marshal Mitchell Slade was staying on in Hatfield, couldn't – or *wouldn't* – say when he might be leaving. This made a lot of folk uneasy. Sure, it was good to know the town was going to be cleaned up but not everyone – in fact, *far from* everyone – even figured Hatfield needed a marshal hanging around, poking his nose into everyone's affairs. Not that anyone said this out loud: if put into words at all, it was done in a whisper behind closed doors, or in some dark, lonely corner where word wasn't likely to reach Slade.

But there wasn't a single resident of Hatfield who would consider pushing their luck and asking Slade just what he hoped to find.

If they had – and *if* Slade had answered – they would've been surprised when the lawman told them he didn't know – only that Sheriff Lew Towney had been under suspicion for a long time and finally someone had been sent to find out just what was going on . . . and *he* was that someone.

It didn't take long to figure Towney was two-faced: in an ideal position to use confidential information that literally fell into his hands as the town's lawman.

Stage schedules; the runs where a strongbox was carried and needed extra guarding – which meant the contents were of high value; movements of bank money and such. . . .

There had been talk, too, about Towney helping men on the dodge find a way into the secret hills of the Humpbacks where they could lose themselves and be beyond the reach of the *genuine* law.

So, *someone* with a conscience had sent word to the federal marshals about the situation and suggested they send a man down to look into things before they worsened and maybe endangered the lives of the citizens of Hatfield.

Slade had sent a wire to the Marshal's Office in Santa Fe requesting the information: *who had sent for the marshal?* but for the answer to be sent to him in code.

The reply came promptly: he wasn't a man who used the marshals' code much, but he was experienced enough to retain some of the letters and their coded combinations in his memory. So when he stared at the reply he held, he was surprised to find his hands beginning to tremble – just a little – but, if he was right, well, it didn't make sense.

For the name that came into his mind when he

tried working out the coded reply from memory was: *Margarita Chavez*, née Towney. . . .

'I would never have contacted them, if – if I'd even suspected they would send someone like *you*!'

Her voice trembled as she almost spat the words at him. Slade kept his face blank, but he could see she was on the verge of tears. All this must be humiliating for her.

He answered calmly, even-voiced, trying to ease the tension.

'Did you know your father was mixed up in the Shuffle? That's what they call the pipeline they use to get outlaws across a State Line, isn't it? For money, of course. A man in your father's position would be mighty valuable and stand to make a good profit for little effort. Is that why you sent for a marshal? To end it before he became involved to the extent that the only way out for him was by exposure and a long jail term, or even a death sentence from some judge? Or did you hate him so much because he had had your husband killed and you wanted to see him disgraced, or maybe even—'

His ears rang and his teeth rattled when her openhanded blow landed and sent him reeling sideways.

'*No, damn you*! I – did – not – *hate* – him! I-I only wanted to throw a scare into him so he – he would stop the stupidity before it got him killed!' Her eyes blazed at Slade. 'But it *did* get him killed when they sent you!'

He could hardly make out her last words: they

were barely intelligible as she choked on emotion, tears running down her face, unheeded, and—

He reached out quickly, caught her around the waist and swung her stumbling body against him, his other arm going around her shoulders and preventing her from falling.

She was limp, not struggling, and he quickly carried her to the small sofa across the room and laid her on it.

He brought her a glass of water, but she was regaining control even as he handed it to her when she struggled to a sitting position. She drank it gratefully. Their gazes met across the glass rim. He spoke quietly.

'I reckon I'm walkin' on dangerous ground here, but if you asked for a marshal, then. . . .' He spread his hands.

'Yes, I know! You're him and I'm responsible for you being here.' Her voice sharpened and her face changed as she added, 'And the first thing you do is k-kill my father!'

She made a marathon effort and swallowed a sob, determined not to break down in front of him again.

He figured she was stronger than she let on, but was still hit mighty hard by what she had done.

'Look, here and now ain't the time to resurrect that.' He lifted a hand quickly, cutting off her reply. 'You know how it happened – and why. There's nothing either of us can do about it. I've already told you I'm sorry it happened – and I meant it – but your father—'

'Oh, stop it!' She briefly covered her ears with her hands, and he saw the deliberate – and powerful – effort she made to try and remain calm. 'I know your favoutite saying: *I am the law*! And . . . and my father used those same words many a time, but he was weak enough to give in to temptation.'

Slade frowned. 'I-I ain't too sure you mean that.'

Her eyes looked momentarily alarmed. 'What would you know? Less than five minutes after you came to town he was lying dead in that saloon.'

He gave her a level stare, then nodded briefly to himself. 'Reckon I'll be gettin' along, ma'am. I won't be telling anyone was you sent for me.'

'I didn't send for *you*! I sent for a *lawman*, but *they* sent a killer!'

He was at the door now and had his hand on the knob when she said. 'You don't even know *why* he broke his law officer's oath.'

Slade frowned. 'There was no time to ask,' he said tightly and turned the knob, but her next words stopped him.

'My mother . . . died of cancer about six months ago.'

He released the knob, turned and leaned his wide shoulders against the door. 'You've had it rough, but—'

'I don't want your sympathy!' Her voice was shaking a little now but he saw she was determined to have her say. He felt uneasy but more than curious: it was obvious to him she wanted to get whatever it was off her chest but why she would choose him – of all people – he had no idea.

It was sad enough in its way, but also foolish – mighty foolish – though he could savvy how desperation drove Lew Towney to taking that fatal step which made him that most detested of badge-toters: a lawman who could be bought.

The news was devastating to both the sheriff and his estranged daughter: their wife and mother had been diagnosed with that most dreaded and incurable of all diseases, *cancer*.

There was vague hope occasionally when charlatans appeared out of whatever worm-ridden holes where they dwelt and preyed upon the inconsolable and desperate kinfolk.

Both Margarita and Lew Towney were sceptical but conscience would not allow them to say no to every such offer. And then there *was* some real hope: Dorothea Towney's condition showed a sudden, though slight, improvement.

Any medical man, even at that time, could have dashed their hopes by telling them that it was not an actual improvement but what was termed a remission when the cancer apparently responded to treatment, but in every such case it was no more than temporary.

The poor, hopeful kinfolk of the patient, grabbing at *any* vague and apparent improvement were, in most cases, mighty hard to convince and suffered even more when the condition flared up again, and often more aggressively.

But during that first surge of unreasoning expectation they would do anything – *anything*! – for the unexpected chance that *here might be the long sought-after breakthrough.*

'It – it was a terribly worrying, and yet hopeful time,' Margarita told him, her voice edged with inconsolable grief. 'My father would not have it any other way than that this time the miracle really was happening—'

'Providing he could keep on coming up with the dollars necessary for the new treatment?' Slade asked heavily, feeling a surge of hatred beginning to grow within him: hatred for the vultures who preyed on the gullibility of distressed people in such circumstances.

It was easy to guess what she was going to say: Lew Towney was willing to take *any* chance that would help his wife. So, to keep the necessary and growing fees coming, he learned it was simple and profitable to peddle information about stageline shipments of payrolls or bank money, complete with schedules and routes planned – and then McKendrick, a man always looking for more ways to increase his own income, put out feelers about the Shuffle, the movement of men on the dodge to hideouts on safe escape routes – for a cost – a *high* cost at times.

'*I won't help any rapists, child-molesters, wife-killers or the like,*' *Lew Towney had insisted – and he had kept his word: money from helping other law-breakers who were 'shuffled' down the escape pipeline – his share of the profits – he passed on to the 'healers' who were treating his ailing wife. . . .*

And *successfully*, they assured him. . . .

The girl was looking distressed now, but she made an effort to finish. 'Of course there was no cure for my mother's condition, not even any real improvement. And, as I said, she died about six months ago.'

Her voice began to break and Slade held up a hand.

'I've come across such cases before.' There was a grimness to his tone and the way his features hardened. 'Your father was a fool, but it's easy to say so, standing at this distance.' He paused, made sure she was looking at him, and added, 'I have to tell you again: it was he who tried to kill *me*. I acted in self-defence.'

'I know, I *know*!' she said, her voice breaking a little. 'I-I'm not altogether stupid!' She tossed her head, hair flying briefly. 'It still isn't anything I can forgive you for!' She paused and looked – *tortured*, he figured was the word that fit best. 'And I can't forgive myself!'

He frowned, started to ask what she meant, but she shook her head quickly.

'I-I meant for causing my father's death,' she said with a rush, the tears welling again. 'We'd *almost* reconciled after Mother died, but if I hadn't interfered, thinking that the presence of a marshal might make him give up the illegal dealings he was involved in—'

'He kept on even after your mother died?' Slade asked, surprised.

She nodded. 'Like I said, the money came easily, *too* easily, and he wasn't well himself – some chest complaint. He was a heavy smoker, too, and he had developed a . . . liking for whiskey, so I wanted to get him away from here. I thought that the presence of a marshal might make him realize just how dangerous it was for him to continue the way he was going. And I'd hoped to be able to talk whoever they sent down into not prosecuting him and ruining his career entirely. I didn't expect to come up against someone like you!'

That was enough: her shoulders shook and her jaw trembled as she tried to control a rising sob.

She wouldn't look at him now.

'Fair enough. Thanks for telling me. Too bad you didn't contact the federal marshals sooner: it might've come out a little differently.'

Her eyes seemed to pinch down a little as she battled with her clamouring conscience.

'I'm sure it would've!' she said crisply. 'They might've sent someone who wasn't as quick on the trigger as you!'

He turned the doorknob and opened it partly, looking over his shoulder at the pale girl.

'Well, that seems to be the end of this conversation.' As he closed the door behind him he added, 'Goodnight to you.'

He heard the first sob wrenched from deep within her, then strode away quickly, face grim as a hangman's.

It may have turned out to be a pretty good night for Margarita Chavez (née-Towney), but not so for US Marshal Mitchell Slade.

Her house – or, rather her late father's house – was set a little aside from the other three or four dwellings in Cannon Street, and there was a stretch of vacant land between the Towney place and its neighbour.

Slade walked it alertly – a long-ingrained habit – and was drawing almost level with the picket fence of the nearest neighbour when he heard the sound . . . behind him.

No hesitation: he whirled, beginning the gunman's crouch, the Colt almost free of leather, and then something like a falling tree hit him.

Because he was beginning his crouch, the savage blow glanced off his shoulders. He stumbled, going down to all fours, hands instinctively lowering to save himself. In a life-saving, automatic reaction, he allowed himself to drop instantly. This lessened the blow in part but still sent his hat skidding. He heard the gusting breath of his attacker even as he started to roll on to his back, trying to ignore the already throbbing, burning pain across his upper back.

The gun came free, but because his arm was numb he dropped it and then the shadows closed in – three of them at least, he figured later. He rolled away, turned it into a series of spins and put some distance between himself and the trio intent on . . . *what?* Killing him? A bullet would be quicker and allow them escape time, but there seemed little point in knocking him senseless and leaving him.

But, of course, there were more ways than one to knock a man senseless, and the billet of wood that had cracked him across the shoulders whistled down towards his head again. He was still moving from his rolling manoeuvre and increased it abruptly, kicking out. Someone began to howl and dance as his boot raked vulnerable shins. He kept rolling and a man cursed as the length of wood struck the ground and jarred up the swinger's arms.

Slade was flat on his back now, lifted both legs, swiftly, hard. They connected with a second man who started to swear but swallowed the curse and let go a howl of pain instead.

Slade thrust up and the third man's shoulder took him under the jaw and sent him staggering. He did a strange dance in an effort to keep balance, as someone kicked his legs out from under, and he went down again.

'Lemme . . . *at* . . . the sonuver!' a man gasped and the wood whistled down again.

'Christ! Don't kill him!' a voice ordered.

Well, that was something! Slade thought, the words streaming through his whirling senses. *They weren't going to kill him – No! Just* cripple *him.*

'*No, thank you!*'

He didn't know for sure whether he shouted the words aloud or only in his head, but he wasted no time in making his attempt to get out of this less-than-expert beating.

His reaching hands touched the billet of wood – smooth, so it was likely a wagon-wheel spoke or axe handle. In any case there were no splinters to tear at his hands as he closed them around the wood and heaved, throwing himself backwards. There were startled yells and he felt the length of wood in his own grasp as he twisted like a pretzel and got unsteadily to his feet. He was swinging before he was balanced and although he missed, heard the whistling sound of the weapon as he put real effort into it. His attackers jumped back too, trying to get out of reach.

One of them fell and a second man tripped over him, though didn't go down: Slade didn't wait to check and he had dropped the third man before he realized another was on his feet again . . . and behind him.

He came around swinging but a rifle barrel cracked across the side of his head and he went down to one knee, dropping the length of wood. Lights spun and swirled and he made a deep rasping sound in his throat, put out his hands as he began to fall.

In a crouching position, swaying, he felt the first boot bend his ribs and yelled involuntarily. The next kick skidded off his head and there were bright red flashes and alternating patches of darkness.

'*Now*!' a voice grunted. '*Get him!*'

Slade felt he was already got but they hadn't really started.

He went out quickly, not all that deeply, and not enough to prevent him feeling the pain as they kicked and stomped, and leaned down and played a mighty painful tattoo up and down his back with that *same goddamn piece of wood*!

He felt himself going out all the way, ready to slip

over the edge of the pit of darkness that was opening around him. . . .

'Get away from him! I said get away!'

The words came and went inside his roaring head and then there was the crash of a shotgun and he winced, fell on his face in the dust, and just lay there, blinking, feeling like he had just barely survived a cattle stampede, waiting to see where he eventually woke up.

But he passed out all the way even as someone tried to help him to his feet.

His head bounced off the ground this time and he was only vaguely aware that now he was being dragged somewhere, boots trailing in the dust.

Then there was nothing but starless night.

CHAPTER 6

SWORN ENEMIES?

'Damn! I thought I must be dreaming! Though, by God, the aches an' pains are real enough.'

Margarita Chavez started back as he spoke, the damp piece of gauze dripping on the left side of his gravel-scarred face. 'I'm glad they gave up when they did.'

'I don't think they were *really* trying,' she said curtly. 'I believe they were reluctant to kill you, but. . . .'

He lifted one stiff and sore hand with swollen knuckles, almost slipping off the edge of the same sofa where he had placed her earlier. 'That was you – with the shotgun?'

'Yes – a double-barrelled one.' She tilted her chin a little, eyes looking at him steadily. 'Someone recommended it, in case I got too excited and missed with the first shot.'

He stared back at her and then said, 'Sounds like good advice. But better be careful: your lips twitched then. Could almost mistake it for a smile – *al-most.*'

'Unintended,' she told him shortly and, as she straightened, he saw the deep yellow-brown colour of the cloth pad she had been using and recognized the ubiquitous iodine.

'You dragged me back here?' She barely nodded. 'And painted me with that stuff?' His words slurred and he touched his face, looking at the yellow stain on his fingertips. 'Well, I thank you for bringing me here – might have to think about this war paint, though.'

She tried to keep a straight face, cocked her head on one side. 'Mmm. You do look kind of like an Apache about to go on a raid.'

He moaned and moved his body gently. 'Feel more like I've already been – and the palefaces won.'

This time she smiled, even chuckled.

'I'm sorry – no, *really*! But you have so much skin scraped off from where you fell . . . you needed antiseptic.'

'Lady, I didn't *fall*, I was pushed! Dropped, if you like. *Kicked*, would be even more accurate.'

'Well, you seem chipper enough now, surprisingly, so I guess you can leave whenever you want to. Though it would probably be a good idea to see a doctor: Doc Harris is only two streets along. Last house. Large property.'

He shook his head gently as he eased up straighter. 'Gotta go look for my gun: it fell outa the holster.'

Her face set in more serious lines as she turned away, went to a shelf and took down something wrapped in part of a used flour sack. She thrust it almost in his face.

'You and your damned guns! As if they'll help you heal from the beating! I found it. Here, take it. I thought you'd want it back – your tool of trade, I suppose you'd call it?'

'That's what it is.' He took the weapon, unwrapped it and wiped the deadly contours with the piece of flour sack, ridding it of any dust and grit, the deep-blue metal gleaming. His hands were shaking and he fumbled as he opened the cylinder and spun it. He snapped his head up.

'It's no damn good empty!'

She turned to the same shelf and passed him the cartridges she had removed. He fumbled them twice but managed to push them one by one into the cylinder. After a pause, he snapped it closed, spun it to make sure it revolved smoothly, and put it into the holster he was still wearing.

'Feel better now?'

He nodded. 'Like havin' an old friend back.'

'I wouldn't think a man like you would have many friends.'

'Here we go again!' he sighed, looking at her steadily. 'Let's not start scrapping. I'm mighty grateful to you for what you've done and I-I—'

She frowned as he stumbled, any words lost in an incoherent mumble. 'You're not as tough as you make out, you know. . . . You look terrible. You *should*

61

see a doctor.'

He detected actual concern in her voice but his gaze never wavered. He was surprised to find how tightly he was holding on to the arm of the sofa: *afraid of falling off?*

'I had a passing thought – just after those fellers jumped me, that—' He stopped, shrugged. 'Ah, never mind. It was stupid. Better left unsaid.'

'You'd better sit down again!' She looked tight about the lips, her stare icy as he pulled his arm away from her steadying grip. 'You thought I might have arranged your ambush! *Didn't you!*'

Hesitating, he nodded. 'Crossed my mind.' Seeing her face tighten even more, he added hastily, 'But I wasn't thinking clearly at that stage – wasn't even fully conscious. I'm glad I thought wrong.'

'You were wrong to come here at all in my view.'

'I think I can savvy how you must feel.'

'Oh, *can* you! Well, I don't think you have even one damn *notion* about how I feel!'

He let her words hang for a few moments, swaying.

'Well, bad as that must be, Margaret, you were still decent enough to rescue me from those— *Now* what's wrong, for God's sake!'

Bracing himself against the wall, he broke off what he was going to say because of the almost *stunned* look on her face. He frowned more deeply when he saw tears sliding down her cheeks. 'I better be going,' he murmured a little desperately. *Damn! He never had understood women, much, but this one had him properly buffaloed.*

'He always called me Margaret, never Margarita: he hated anything that had a Mexican sound. . . .'

Slade nodded. 'You mean your father, of course? OK. Look, I'm too fumble-footed to stay here right now. We're gonna be at loggerheads again, any minute. You have my thanks: I'm mighty grateful. . . . So, goodnight again.' He hesitated as he began to turn, quite dizzy, but trying to hide it. 'You – will you be OK here? I mean, those skunks must know where you came from.'

She reached in beside a tall cupboard and brought out the double-barrelled Greener shotgun. 'Then they also know I still have this.'

He nodded, and, with a tight-lipped smile, touched a pair of fingers to his battered hat, which he picked up off a chair and settled on his throbbing head. It sat high because of the bandage and swelling from being hit with the piece of timber. He pushed it back a little.

'Would you like to borrow this?' she asked, perhaps with a suggestion of levity in her words, although her face was serious as she proffered the shotgun.

'Some other time maybe. . . . You happen to catch a glimpse of whoever jumped me?'

She frowned, seemed about to shake her head, then said, 'I did – and I didn't, if you know what I mean.'

'I ain't thinking that good. But I got me a good idea who it was, anyway.'

'I did catch a glimpse of them when I fired the

63

shotgun, but they were right at the very edge of the flash so I can't be sure. One looked ordinary enough – you know, average tall and so on – but the other . . . it must've been a trick of the light, I suppose.'

'*What* was?' he asked, impatience obvious in his tone and attitude.

Her frown deepened as she told him. 'I-I thought the second one was just a *boy*! I know, I know that must sound crazy, but he looked no bigger than a schoolboy – about ten or twelve years— *Oh!*' His face had hardened. 'Don't tell me you actually *do know* someone like that?'

She could read it in his battered face and his mouth lifted in a crooked smile. 'Yeah, I know the son of a bitch, *and* his sidekick.'

'And, of course, you're being stupid and going to – look for them – *now*? With a bleeding gash in the back of your head and—'

'Seems as good a time as any. They might even still be hangin' around, hoping to finish the job.'

'And you're going to give them the chance. Are you mad? This time they *will* kill you!'

'Could've finished me earlier, several times. They've got enough sense to know you don't *kill* a US Marshal and plan for your old age, but it's OK to beat the daylights outa him in the hope of frightening him off.'

'And, of course, *that's* a vain hope.'

'It can happen, but not with me.'

'Of course not. You're crazy enough to go after them with – with possible concussion, bruised, if not cracked, ribs and – and – I suppose "various other injuries" would cover it! Marshal or not, I think you're a damned fool!'

Once again he touched two fingers to the brim of his hat. 'Likely you're right, but— For now, as we say in Texas: *muchas gracias* and *buenos noches, señorita.* Oh, and *adios.*'

He loosened the six-gun in the holster and, as he was about to move off, saw her puzzled face. 'What?'

She gestured to the gun. 'On that metal – strap, I suppose you'd call it, the one on the butt, between the plates—?'

Frowning, he waited. 'Yeah—?'

'There are two initials engraved into the metal, very fancy, but I think I read them right – C and R. There's no way I can make them into *your* initials.'

'They stand for Cass Richman. You might know the name.'

Her puzzlement was stronger than ever. 'There was a notorious outlaw and killer called that – up in one of the Dakotas, I think—'

'South Dakota. He favoured the country around Deadwood. Which was where we ran into each other.' He took the gun out and turned it in his hands several times, then looked at her. 'Cass don't need it any more.'

Her mouth tightened. 'Oh, I guessed that! You killed him for it, of course.'

'He was trying to kill me with it.'

'Do you usually keep souvenirs of the men you shoot?'

He half-smiled, shook his head. 'This is a special Colt. One made in England, under licence. I dunno how Cass came by it but he was pretty much an educated man for the kind of trade he followed. Told me once the Limeys' metal was superior to ours, even that used by the original Colt factories here. It does feel different: tolerances are better, too, so the parts move a lot more smoothly and the foresight's hooded to protect it from damage. So, yeah, in this case I kept it.'

'Because, as you said, he had no more use for it.'

He held her angry gaze for a brief moment, then nodded, said quietly, 'I'll be going now,' and went out of the room.

She heard the front door close behind him, looked at the shotgun she still held and put it back beside the cupboard before sitting down in a straightback chair.

What the devil was she doing? This was the man who had killed her father – and here she was helping him.

But there was something about him, she admitted to herself, reluctantly, a kind of straightness, no nonsense, so that you knew exactly where you stood with him.

Maybe it was honesty, or courage, or even decency.

'*In a cold-blooded killer?*' she asked herself softly. 'You damned little fool!'

And then there was a crash outside on the short set of steps leading to the street: a kind of confused clatter followed by a thump.

66

'Oh, my God!'

She ran to the door and wrenched it open, looking down at the huddled heap of Mitchell Slade, motionless at the foot of the steps.

This time he knew where he was – maybe not *exactly*, but he had been in enough doctors' infirmaries to recognize the usual clutter and the glistening chromework of medical paraphernalia, shelves of bottles with strange words on the labels, and the stink of medication and anaesthetic, in fact, the choking stench – *and taste?* – of chloroform. The headache between his eyes made him want to get out of here, pronto.

A pair of gnarled, veiny and age-spotted hands came into the ambit of his vision and firmly pushed against his upper chest. 'Back – back – *back*, I said, dammit!'

He gave up fighting the pressure and flopped down, tried to talk – or curse – the not yet clearly seen sawbones, but his throat felt numb and he reckoned *he'd* been given chloroform not so long ago.

His vocal sounds were no better than those of a disoriented and frightened animal. The hands came back and this time they really pushed, pressing him down against the pillows and the mattress.

'Oh, shut *up*!' growled a cranky voice from the shadows somewhere above the gnarled hands. 'Just lie back and be *quiet*! Or I'll give you a whiff of chloroform this time that'll put you into the middle of next week!'

He sagged. 'OK, Doc. You're the boss.'

That's what he *thought* he said, *wanted* to say, but it came out in a tumble of gibberish and the croaky voice said, quite disinterestedly. 'Yes, yes, of course – whatever you said. I *agree* with you. You're a very smart fellow. Now just be a *co-operative* one as well, and we'll get along fine. I'm Doctor Harris, by the way.'

Slade's woozy mind didn't register his left hand slightly lifting in acknowledgement, but the surprise that he *had* understood was clear in Harris's voice.

'Well, well! I do believe we have ourselves a true tough one here! It seems a long time since I've run up against someone like that. *Are* you tough, Marshal?'

'Whatever the hell you say, Doc, I'll go along with you.'

His words were slurred, but understandable, and he had a strange feeling of – contentment? – or something like it, right now.

Those were his thoughts as he happily drifted off into his half-drugged world again.

His battered mouth even moved in a semblance of a smile. Maybe his dreams were more pleasant than the reality.

The next time he opened his eyes it was dark and it took quite some time before he could make out his surroundings.

His brain was – *foggy*. Yeah, that'd do to describe it. Still, he knew he was in the same place as before, the

68

infirmary, but with the taste of that lousy chloroform now slightly diminished yet still there to some degree.

'Thank God it's gradually goin'!'

He said that out loud, fumbled on the bedside table for a glass of water he remembered – his thirst was *monumental*! – but he knocked it over and it rolled off, broke with a loud crash.

After a few minutes there was a glow showing beneath a nearby door, which opened, and a stooped man came in holding a burning candle in a metal holder.

'Ah! Conscious again at last?' the remembered cranky voice asked, though *not* so irritable now. 'I was beginning to worry that I'd given you an overdose.'

Slade understood perfectly, heard every word, and the fogginess seemed to have left his brain now that he was properly conscious. He smacked his dry, scaly lips and growled some words that he couldn't understand.

'You'll be very thirsty,' the sawbones said. 'It's a natural after-effect. But I had to give you quite a bit of anaesthetic while I tended your shoulders and, more importantly, your head wound. If it would interest you, I had to put seven sutures in a quite deep cut on the back of your head. You must've given it quite a wallop.'

Slade gulped greedily as the gnarled old hands held a glass of water to his lips.

'Not too fast!' snapped the medic. 'You'll make yourself sick and it's too far past my bedtime for me to have the chore of cleaning *that* up! The water can stay but— Ah! That's better: just sip. Your thirst will pass soon enough.'

Slade didn't know how long it took, but he felt way better before the glass was two-thirds empty. The doctor took it from him and placed it on a small table where the candle, in its holder, burned slowly.

'Margarita did well to insist you come here instead of chasing some drunks she said attacked you. Is that right?'

'They weren't drunk, Doc. And she likes to be called Margaret.'

'Uh-ha! So you have already reached that point! It's a wonder to me she didn't poison your food. She was very close to her father, you know.'

'Don't you start! But, yeah, I got that impression. Where'd you put my clothes, Doc?'

The candlelight highlighted all the deep creases and wrinkles of the medic's face. He had a large beak of a nose and grey whiskers which followed the outline of his jaw, but he did not sport a moustache. He shook his head slowly.

'I do believe we have something of a comedian here, don't we?'

'Not me, Doc. I just want my clothes so I can get outa here. I've got an expense account I can draw on through your local bank so you'll be paid as soon as I'm on my feet. Hey! Where the hell you goin'?'

'Back to bed where I ought to be.' Doc Harris paused with his hand on the doorknob. 'There will be a nurse look in on you from time to time during the night and I must warn you, she is not only strong, but has visited the Mysterious Orient and knows swift – and painful – nerve holds which bring even the biggest and roughest to their knees, begging for mercy.'

'Hell, with that! I have to get out of here . . . but I'll need my gun.'

Slade kicked and fussed with the bedclothes, surprised how taut they were drawn over him and how hard it was to move. He glanced up and swore; the candlelight glistened off the big teeth as the medic peeled his lips back in a smirk.

'I kid you not, Marshal. Shall I call the nurse? Or will you show some sense and take a sleeping draught I've prepared for you? Believe me, you'll feel the benefit of it in the morning.'

In truth, Slade did not feel so chipper right now and his head thundered like the worst hangover he could remember.

So he sighed heavily and growled, 'All right! Gimme the damn draught – and put a slug of redeye in it as well, OK? But I'd be a lot happier *if you'd bring me my damn gun!*'

That cranky old voice sounded like a broody hen cackling, Slade thought savagely, as the sawbones went to a cupboard and came to stand by the bed again, holding the Colt in its holster.

'A special gun, eh? But it looks like any ordinary pistol I've ever seen.'

Slade felt suddenly wary. 'What makes you think it's different?'

71

'Did I say that? I thought I said 'special' Mmm. The metal does have a different look from other Colts I've seen. The candlelight seems to reflect back more deeply, from *within* the blueing. I'm rather interested in unusual weapons. Would you consider selling this to me? Perhaps trading it for the cost of your treatment here?'

There were all kinds of strange thoughts and notions whirling around in Mitchell Slade's throbbing head. But he couldn't separate them from the slightly unreal feeling he had, as if he was floating just above his mattress. It was more than likely just a hangover from the chloroform – he hoped! – and wouldn't last long.

He started chuckling, involuntarily, so he knew he wasn't *quite* out of the last of the anaesthetic's effects yet. 'You that hard up for patients?' Slade gave a short laugh, out loud this time. 'You gotta haul 'em in at gunpoint?'

'Oh, very funny! Now, go back to sleep and be damned to you! *And* your renegade's gun!'

The old doctor flung the weapon back into the cupboard drawer as he went out, taking the candle with him.

Strangely, Slade welcomed the resulting darkness that inevitably enfolded him. Quickly. . . .

CHAPTER 7

WARM NIGHT

'I'm gonna kill the son of a bitch, no matter what they say!'

Big Jock's voice was higher than normal and Red Connor felt some apprehenson when he saw that ugly little face contort, the way it did when he was torturing some helpless ranny – or, preferably, woman. No! Make that girl: Jock always preferred 'em young – younger the better, even school kids. . . .

Red had never asked why and never would. He was pretty sure he knew the answer but would never mention it, not unless he was crazy-drunk and felt like dying.

But this announcement of Big Jock's required an answer and he knew better than to take a lecturing tone when the small man was in this kind of mood.

'You do and you might's well shove your Colt in your mouth and pull the trigger. No! You listen to me, Jock! I don't have to tell you *why*! Goddammit, you wouldn't be able to *move* for all the marshals they'd send in here! And everyone of 'em would have the unofficial order to *kill the bastard who was loco enough to pull the trigger on one of their own*!'

'But, hell, Red! It's such a perfect chance! I mean, we already missed one chance when that gal dragged him back to her place after nearly blowin' our heads off. I listened to you then, but— We got a second go now that he's in Harris's infirmary. There's only a couple other patients, and Slade's all alone in a back room.'

'Goddammit, Jock!' Connor snapped, feeling the taste of bile in his throat. He was really worked up about this but his heart was thundering, for he had seen his diminutive companion go off the rails a few times and shoot everyone – *everyone* – in sight and to hell with the consequences.

But – *no*! Red Connor just couldn't take the risk. *Hell! What risk?* There was no doubt as to what the retaliation would be for the murder of a federal man, and *he* didn't aim to be on that damned 'Vengeance List' he had heard they kept for such occasions.

'Jock, you've gotta listen to me.'

Red blinked when the other looked up at him in silence for a few seconds and then nodded. 'Yeah, yeah, I guess what you say makes sense. Passin' up a damn good chance, though.'

'We'll have our day – or night,' Connor said with unashamed relief in his voice. 'Who knows? He might have a fatal accident, or one of his old enemies might find him and save us the trouble. There's plenty want to see Slade dead.'

'Huh? Oh, yeah, yeah, I s'pose that's possible.' Big Jock seemed to be thinking of something else. 'All right. Let's see if we can get some shut-eye.'

'Hell, I figured we'd quit town tonight. Get the hell outa here while Slade's laid up. I don't want to think about him along my backtrail in *daylight*!'

'Reckon not, daylight or any time.' Jock stifled a yawn. 'But, hell, I'm pooped, anyway. Let's grab a bunk at McKendrick's and we'll leave come sun-up. After that beatin' we give Slade, he won't feel like comin' after us right away, I reckon.'

Red squinted at Big Jock: it wasn't like the man to give in this easy. He was a mighty touchy little *hombre*, but. . . .

'Yeah, OK! Mac mightn't be too happy about puttin' us up after Slade told him to get rid of us, or else.'

They were already walking back to their horses and Connor lifted his hat and scratched at his sweaty head.

He had a notion – a damned *disturbing* notion – that Big Jock had his own agenda and was planning something that would endanger them both.

He was right, as it turned out, but he would never have guessed what Big Jock was up to, and by then it was way, way too late to do anything about it.

'Where the hell you been?' demanded Connor, propping himself up on one elbow in the narrow bunk behind the false wall in McKendrick's toolshed. 'Thought you must've gotten locked in the privy or something.'

Big Jock groped his way towards his bunk.

'Ah, musta ate too much of that Mex grub at the diner. Gimme a bellyache. I'm OK now.'

'Ye-ah, well, you did make somethin' of a hog of yourself. Everythin' all right now?'

'Whatever you mean by "all right" – yeah. So far as my belly's concerned it is. G'night.'

' 'Night. . . .' Red's reply was kind of drawn-out, like he was thinking of something else. But then he lowered himself back into the bunk as he heard Jock pulling up his bedclothes. *He didn't know why he was still so jumpy.*

Red was still rearranging his pillow, still kind of puzzled and uneasy, then finally laid his head down and closed his eyes.

They flew wide open within seconds and he jerked upright. 'Holy Joe! What the *hell's* that?'

Big Jock's puzzled voice came through the darkness. 'Helluva racket! All them bells – an' I think I hear – shoutin' an'— Hey! Somethin's on.'

He flung back the bedclothes and opened the front door. 'Judas Priest!'

'What the hell is it?' Connor asked, pushing the smaller man aside and stepping out into the darkness.

'Hell almighty, it's a fire. Got a good hold, too, and. . . .'

His voice trailed off as Big Jock climbed on to a tree stump at one end of the shed for a better view.

'Man, that is some fire! Damn! I believe it's the doctor's place.'

Doc Harris's big house on its large block of land stood out like a huge, macabre birthday cake as flames engulfed the old timber building.

There were two fire-fighting pump trucks, manned by volunteers, in Hatfield. One had made it as far as the front of Harris's house where the doctor himself was running back and forth along his big front veranda, screaming for help to get some water on the flames before they reached his store of alcohol and the very flammable anaesthetics.

The second fire truck had bogged down at the river crossing and the volunteers were shouting and whipping at the panicked team of horses as they fought the harness.

'Get that second fire wagon up here!' a big man bellowed. 'Or this place'll go up like the original Fourth of July!'

There was a surprisingly large crowd already, but that was understandable: Hatfield was mostly a timber-built town and although Doc Harris's place was on the edge, the way sparks were rising and gyrating in glowing spirals, they could carry the fire to the centre of town itself.

People were already holding blankets and books

and slabs of discarded timber over their heads or in front of their faces as the heat blasted up the slopes.

'By God! I sure wouldn't like to be in there!' someone opined and there was a brief silence, and then a score of voices agreed as the flames surged high, and the heat shattered glass in the windows. Shingles were flying off like missiles, made mobile by the gases generated by the roaring flames.

'Anyone get out?' A woman managed to make herself heard with her query.

'Ain't no one gettin' outa there alive, dearie!' opined a second woman, clutching a gown that covered her nightdress tightly around her throat. 'Whole blamed place is burnin'!'

'Oh, my stars! I had an appointment to see Doc Harris tomorrow about my rheumatiz. It's been givin' me gyp.'

'Myra Castle seen an Injun medicine man and she says he cured her,' a trembly female voice announced.

'Is that right? I hope Myra turns out to see this. Oh, yes! There she is – I'll go ask her the details.'

In the confusion, and amid some muscular swearing, the stuck fire wagon was finally pushed ashore and rushed towards the blaze, which by now seemed to be lighting up half the town. Reflected flames actually made the normally nondescript river look like a large golden serpent, writhing through the night.

There didn't seem to be much left of Doc Harris's fine old house.

Then a male voice raised the question: 'How many

patients did Doc have?'

'Dunno, but I bet he don't have 'em now.'

'What a tragedy. All them folk killed.'

'And *accidentally*, that makes it worse!'

Several heads turned at the words and had to search momentarily to see who had spoken. Then someone lowered his gaze and saw Big Jock was the one.

'*Accidentally*, Jock. . . ?'

'Well, yeah.' The small man gestured to the still-blazing framework of the doctor's house. 'The fire, dunno what caused it, but I s'pose it was an accident?'

'*Hell!* It had better been!'

Red Connor was standing beside Big Jock, towering over the man. 'Whoever was in there died by accident, eh?'

'Gawd! This'll be known as a bad-luck town now!'

'*Yeah*, real bad luck,' opined Big Jock. 'I think someone said that new marshal was in there. Bet not too many of them fellers expect to go by accident, this way.'

Red Connor continued to look down at the small man and then smiled slowly. 'What you might call *mighty* bad luck!'

'Yeah. But I s'pose them hot-shot lawmen run that risk all the time. Though most of 'em go by the bullet—'

'Be quicker,' allowed a bearded man. butting into the group. 'But fire gets you just as dead.'

'S'pose we'll have the town full of lawmen now.'

79

'Why? Nothin' to investigate, is there? Just Slade's bad luck he was laid up in Doc's infirmary when it caught fire. Full stop.'

Big Jock felt Red's gaze upon him and let his own travel quickly over the man's face, just long enough to catch Red's slight nod of approval.

They'd gotten rid of Mitchell Slade and no one could say it was anything but accidental.

Fancy little – pardon! – *Big* Jock having enough brains to figure that out. . . .

In a moment of almost overwhelming enthusiasm, he slapped Big Jock on the back and sent the startled man sprawling.

'Oh, sorry, Jock! Thought you coughed, had somethin' caught in your throat.'

He helped Jock up, began dusting off his clothes, still apologizing. The smaller man glared, then slowly grinned. *Why the hell not?* He'd outsmarted Red and the whole damn Marshals' Service.

'No, Red, I feel fine, just fine.'

CHAPTER 8

LIKE A BREATH
OF HELL

It had been a close call – a very, very close call.

Over the years as a marshal – and even before he pinned on the badge – Mitchell Slade had been wounded several times. Most were surface scratches, as he called them, though many a sawbones had tried to hold him in an infirmary instead of just putting a dressing over the wound as he demanded.

Why he wanted to get in and out of the doctors' places as soon as possible was because he did not like chloroform. He had been given doses of it many a time when deep probing for the bullet in him was necessary, but even a mild dose left him feeling queasy for days.

And so it was during his stay at Doc Harris's now.

He tried to ignore the increasing rumbling of his stomach and finally, sometime late at night, swung his legs over the side of the narrow bed. As far as he was concerned, he was quitting this place come sun-up: he'd been here long enough and felt pretty good, except for this queasiness and a headache. He paused as his bare feet reached the floor.

There was no linoleum or other covering, just smooth planks, with maybe a lick of varnish just to keep any splinters down – so, as usual, he expected the cool, sometimes cold, touch when his feet reached them.

But not this time. The touch was decidedly *warm!* *Warm! Hell, the floor was hot!*

'How in the name of. . . ?' he murmured, moving his feet quickly back and forth, trying several places, each time he felt the heat of the timber and—

Heat! And now – by God, yes! He could smell smoke!

Long living in wooden buildings had made him mighty leery of the smell of smoke until he had located the source: usually coming from the kitchen wood-fired range, or an open fire with smouldering logs, or, a few times, because the place was – *on fire!*

He didn't hesitate, pulled on his boots even as he saw thin tendrils of smoke squeezing up through the minute gaps between the planks. In seconds he had a shirt pulled over his bare torso as he started yelling.

'*Fire! Fire! Get the hell out! Fast!*'

The smell of smoke was strong now, making his nostrils and lips tingle as he lifted the bed and over-turned it, hoping its crashing sound might alert the few other patients and Doc Harris and his wife. He leaned against the wall briefly, dizzy from his efforts.

Someone started yelling wildly from one of the small sections Doc had for the more seriously ill patients, and the sound rapidly became a scream as flames began licking at the window.

Slade, groggy from his head wound, wrenched open the door and leapt back as a wall of fire reached for him. He flung up an arm to protect his face and edged around the licking flames.

'Calm down!' he bawled. 'I'll get you out! Come on, you men! Get moving unless you want to find out how the Sunday roast feels! *Come on, damn you!*'

It was utter chaos: one man, unable to move much, tumbled out of bed and immediately started yelling that he'd just broken his arm.

Doc Harris was in there somewhere – Slade recognized the cracked old voice, weak and almost lost in the racket of the fire and men's curses and the crash and rumble of overturned furniture as the walking wounded made their way into the part of the house that was not yet fully ablaze.

Mrs Harris was screaming and one of the other patients, a man with a busted leg, dragged his plaster cast across to her in a series of thumps. He picked her up and unceremoniously threw her over one shoulder and was surprised when she stopped screaming: likely startled at being manhandled – *literally!* – this way. Somehow he managed to keep from falling down and staggered towards the door.

Mitch Slade fell twice as he dragged a fat man out

83

of the room and only afterward did the marshal find out the man had no trousers on and was bleating his protests like a starving calf.

The mixture of sounds was as upsetting as the flames themselves as far as Slade was concerned: he simply couldn't tell where the cries for help came from.

But he became staggeringly dizzy, turning quickly towards this sound, whirling about as he realized he had been mistaken, twisted to try again. He fell several times, his hands whipping back swiftly from the now obviously burning floorboards.

Someone screamed and the sound was almost obliterated by the crashing of a section of floor that had given way – the luckless man had fallen into the blazing horror that had now taken hold of Doc Harris's house. . . .

Then, somehow, half-blinded by stinging smoke, he found himself outside and dumped the fat man on a grassy slope. He squinted through his fingers at the inferno that was now consuming the house, saw that one of the fire trucks had arived and its crew were doing their best to extinguish the flames with buckets of water, even wet blankets.

A hopeless task, but the intensity of the fire *had* to be reduced or it could send the whole damn town up in smoke. . . . At last, the fire truck's pump started working feebly.

It was over two hours before the last ember had been drowned and one exhausted volunteer fire-fighter turned the wooden bucket upside down and sat on it heavily, head and arms hanging, breath screeching into his scorched lungs.

Doc Harris, singed, his old nightgown burned half off his skinny frame, mopped his red face and now blackened beard. Someone silently handed him an uncorked bottle and he snatched at it, took a l-o-n-g swallow.

'Better'n any medicine you can dispense, eh, Doc?' the bottle's owner said hoarsely. 'No, no, Doc, take another swig. You've earned it. And so's that big marshal, wherever the hell he is. He was moving so fast, running from place to place, shoving folk out of the way of the fire, he was just a blur. Now I can't even see him.'

But Slade was there, already kicking aside smouldering timbers, stomping through the debris where the house had once stood. He stooped, picked up a broken bottle and turned to the sawbones, who was gasping for breath.

'Wouldn't recommend a swig from *this* bottle, Doc, even if it was intact.' He turned so that a small portion of scorched label could be seen. 'Coal oil don't taste as good as whiskey.'

Doc Harris snatched at the bottle. 'Show me that! Good grief! Are you saying that – that s-someone deliberately burned down my house?' The medic gasped, incredulously, outraged.

'That's it, Doc. Damned lucky no one was killed.'

Harris looked more closely at Slade's blackened face and singed hair.

'Lucky because you raised the alarm!'

Slade smiled ruefully. 'I'll never bad-mouth chloroform again,' he said, and his smile widened as he saw all the strange looks the survivors and hastily dressed rubberneckers were giving him. 'Gimme a shot of redeye any day.'

But it was really no smiling matter.

Someone had been meant to die in that blaze.

Slade was pretty sure it was him.

In the rear of the big crowd that had gathered, Red Connor shoved folk aside roughly and reached out to grab Big Jock's hand as he closed the cylinder of his pistol.

Shielding the man with his own body he crowded Big Jock back into the shadows near a slowly smouldering tree.

'Goddammit! The hell you think you're doin'? Put that gun away!' he hissed.

Jock yanked his arm free and his ugly little face squinted as he turned his angry gaze on Connor. 'Get the hell away from me! You see it? Christ, the son of a bitch is still alive! They're makin' a hero out of him!'

'Because he is! Judas, will you stop fightin' me! Or I swear I'll blow your damned head off!'

Red hissed the words through his teeth, still jostling with the smaller man. 'Jock, it was a good idea, a *damned* good idea, but it din' work! No, listen, you stubborn sonuver. . . . It's too damn late to do anything about it now! *Listen, for Chris'sakes! You go after Slade now and shoot him, you're dead! Look at all*

*these folk – they'll all be witnesses it was you shot him!
You're a goner before you even touch that trigger!'*

Jock glared up at Connor, looked past his shoulder
and saw some of the crowd looking over their way.
He sighed and let it drift into a whispered curse as he
rammed his gun back into the holster. 'All right, all
right, goddammit! But Slade's a dead man! If there's
no other way to do it, I'll shoot him and to hell with
the marshals! They can send in an army of 'em for all
I care.'

Connor held him by one shoulder. 'Talkin' about
the army, they *could* send in a troop and declare
martial law and where the hell would that leave us?'

Big Jock blinked. 'I-I never thought of that. That'd
be the last thing we need. . . . Aw, but I just *gotta* get
that Slade, Red!'

'We'll have to, right enough, but I think we better
wait our chance. Long as we get him outa the way for
when Brazos gets here. . . .'

Little Mister Big Jock nodded solemnly and finally
put his gun back into its holster.

He was still glaring at Mitchell Slade, who watched
deadpan. Jock obviously felt uneasy and Slade took
tobacco sack and papers from his shirt pocket and
rolled a cigarette. He put it between his lips and
patted his pockets, seeing Big Jock straighten
another inch or so – about the man's limit.

Then the marshal strolled across and nodded,
saying, 'Haven't got a match, have you. . . ?'

'Here, I have,' spoke up Red Connor, feeling in his
shirt pocket.

'I'm asking him.' Slade didn't even look at Red and Jock flushed, took a vesta from his pocket and snapped it into flame on his thumbnail, thrust it up near Slade's face, stretching to do it.

'This is a match, Marshal, an' this is how you light it. Thought a man like you'd know how.'

Slade reached out suddenly and grabbed the smaller man's wrist, resisting the instinctive pull, dipped his head and applied the flame to his cigarette. He stepped back, Jock's face red now, not sure how to react.

'Thanks. Thought you might carry a vesta or two.' He looked around and gestured to the still-smoking ruins.

Red Connor snapped angrily, 'You accusin' Jock of somethin'?'

'Red, if I was, I'd say it out loud: like I think he might be the one set fire to Doc's house. . . .'

'Why you—!' Jock could hardly speak he was so incensed and Red moved in quickly and stepped between Slade and Jock.

'Take it easy, Jock. He's ridin' you 'cause he dunno what else to do.'

'He – he can *go for his gun, goddammit*!'

'Jock, *no*!' yelled Connor, trying to grab him more firmly, but the small man jumped to one side, bringing up his Colt in a fast, smooth draw.

Slade shot him once in the chest and the strike of the lead lifted Big Jock and flung him back almost three feet. He hit the ground hard and rolled once, then was still – forever.

Connor had his own gun half-drawn but when Slade's smoking weapon swung towards him he let the weapon drop back into his holster and lifted his hands shoulder high.

'OK! I ain't buyin' into this!'

'Got more brains than I thought,' Slade opined and holstered his gun.

There was a lot of talk among the crowd now, most staring at him, not sure how to react.

'You deliberately forced that man into going for his gun!'

Slade turned to look at Margaret Towney, her face white with anger, small hands clenched at her sides. 'You're as much a killer as you claim he was!'

'I'm also the law.'

'And that, I suppose, gives you the right to—'

Slade interrupted her, voice angry. 'The right to make my own decisions . . . on the spot and *fast*!'

'Whether they're right or wrong?' the girl snapped.

But Slade didn't get a chance to answer.

'Damn you, mister!' gritted Red Connor. 'Jock was my pard for more'n ten years!'

'Mean little so-and-so, wasn't he?'

Red started to react then froze again, shaking his head. 'Ah, no you don't! You ain't ridin' me into drawin'!'

'Suit yourself, Red, but you'd be wise to forget whatever it was you and Big Jock had planned.'

'Who says we had anythin' planned?'

'Why, you just heard me say so, Red. Did I offend

89

you? If I did. . . .' Slade spread his arms invitingly.

Red started to bristle, then paused, and shook his head. 'Ah, to hell with you! We'll square up some other time.'

'I'll watch my back while I'm waiting, Red.'

Connor almost went for his gun then, but common sense prevailed and he swung away, thrusting roughly through the crowd.

'Better send the undertaker for Jock,' Slade called and looked at the uneasy crowd. Margaret Towney was staring at him as if he was a stranger.

'You— I've said it before and I'll say it again: you're as big a killer as the men you hunt down!' she told him shakily.

'My boss thinks so, too: why he sends me. Now, you folk, instead of standing around gawking, oughta pitch right in and get some of this mess cleared up for Doc. He's looked after you for years, an' now he's the one needing help. *Come on! Roll up your sleeves and get started!'*

He gave his Colt an extra push down into his holster and set the example by rolling his sleeves up above his elbows and began throwing some of the blackened timber aside.

Within a few minutes, most of the male population of Hatfield were doing the same while Doc Harris watched in surprise – but with gratitude.

His gaze sought out Slade and he nodded his thanks.

'Much obliged, Marshal.'

Slade turned abruptly as he felt a hand on his arm

and looked down to see Margaret Towney beside him.

'I spoke hastily – I'm sorry. If you have nowhere to go, perhaps you'd like to spend the rest of the night in that spare room I have.'

He smiled slowly. 'Better watch your reputation.'

'Let me worry about that.' As she started to turn away she said, 'You're a man full of surprises, Marshal. I have a darned difficult time making up my mind about you.'

'It's easy: what you see is what you get.'

'I'm beginning to realize that.'

He didn't say anything for a few moments, then waved a hand casually.

'I'll maybe look in when I finish here.'

'Suit yourself,' she said, a mite stiffly.

He smiled to himself, as he started forward to help the others.

CHAPTER 9

BRAZOS

She took a long time to answer the door although he could see a light in the rear of the house.

'So you decided to come after all?' she said as the door opened a crack.

'Aimed to all along – just thought it might be better if I didn't seem too eager.'

She frowned slightly, stood aside as he entered. She was holding a lantern and led the way into her kitchen. A coffee pot was heating on the stove and he thought her cheeks flushed some as she said, 'I decided I wanted a cup of coffee – then, as you said you *might* call in, I made a whole pot. Can I pour you a cup?'

'I'd be obliged.' *She'd really been expecting, or hoping, he would come.*

He sat down and she brought him a cup. He waved away the sugar bowl and the small jug of cream, sipped and obviously burned his lips. He glared as she smiled.

'Don't be in too much of a hurry; there's time to let it cool.'

'Good to know,' he acknowledged slowly.

A short silence stretched into a couple of minutes.

'We don't seem to hit it off too well.' He held up a hand quickly. 'I know it's awkward, me having tangled with your father and so on.'

'It's more than "awkward", but—' She looked down into her coffee, turned the cup slowly between her hands: he guessed it was a lot cooler than his, which meant she had been sitting here for some time – waiting for him?

Maybe.

'Do we have to—?' she began, paused and then said, 'I can't make up my mind about you. You seem so . . . hard, yet you're not uncaring, and you have a sense of obligation.'

'I have?'

'Yes. The way you reminded those people in no uncertain manner how much the doctor had given them over the years and yet it took you – a total stranger – to make them realize that here was an opportunity in some small way, to show some appreciation – of what the whole town must owe Doc Harris.'

'Well, yeah, did seem they needed a little push.'

They sipped coffee and he ate two cookies that she brought on a plate, likely home made. He crunched and nodded.

'You approve?'

'Don't try to be modest! You must know you're a good cook.'

She looked at him a trifle coolly. 'My efforts are generally palatable.' Then abruptly her face changed: as if she had decided, enough with the manners. Let's get down to brass tacks!

'Why did you come here, to Hatfield? Oh, I know it had to do with my father and his – practices – but you don't seem in any hurry to leave. . . . Am I being out of order?'

'I'm waiting for someone.'

'Oh. Well, I guess that's none of my business.'

'It could be everyone's business.' She looked quizzical. 'You ever heard of Brazos McGraw?'

She frowned, then nodded. 'Most folk up here have. He's a-a terrible man. Cold-blooded killer, a rapist, thief. Well, you think of anything criminal and I'm sure somewhere you'll find McGraw's name connected with it.'

'You're right. He's coming here.'

She stiffened. 'Here? You mean to Hatfield?'

'I do. He's aiming to use the Pipeline.'

'I-I don't understand.' Her voice was slowly hardening. 'You used that name when you were trying to explain my father's involvement in this so-called escape route that gets outlaws away to some sort of safety.'

'Right again. All done for a price, of course.'

Her mouth tightened a little more. 'I believe you mentioned something about that, too – after telling

94

me about my father's interest in it, even long after Mother had died of cancer.'

He saw she was breathing faster and it showed in the way she spoke. She reached for her coffee; he noticed her hand was trembling and she didn't pick up the cup – in case she spilled it?

He held her cool, now disturbed, gaze.

'You explained how Lew got involved in the whole deal, and I accept that.'

'Damned good of you!'

'Easy now! Give me a chance to explain: you *did* ask. . . .'

She took a deep, steadying breath. 'All right.'

He paused until he saw the impatience clawing in her and said abruptly, 'This Brazos McGraw, he's a man I've wanted to kill for years – many years.'

Her lips parted a little now and the frown lines between her watchful eyes deepened, but she didn't speak.

'You already know he's one of the meanest snakes ever to live on this earth: he's killed men and women of all ages – children, too. He's indifferent as to who he murders at the time as long as he makes his money, or satisfies some kinda mean streak in him.'

He paused, rolled a cigarette, and she brought him a vesta from a box above the wood range. He fired up. 'He's a sadist, none of his victims dies quickly. I've been after him for too many years.' He paused, seemed to consider, then added, 'Long before he murdered my wife and two-year-old son.'

'Oh! Dear God! You— You must—'

'It's something you never get over.' He took two long drags at his cigarette before continuing. 'I was a lawman at the time, just a town sheriff. I joined the marshals after the funerals, so I'd have a legal right to follow that bastard McGraw anywhere in the country. Couple of years ago, I cornered him but my chief pulled me off. Reckoned it wouldn't reflect well on the Service the way I'd finish off Brazos. He was right, I guess, but a couple of other marshals jumped him and some misguided do-gooders bought into it when he came to trial and they stuck him in jail – for life. Why the hell he didn't hang, I don't know, but that's what happened. Oh, he had a mighty hard time in the Comstock Pen, but he also had a lot of stolen cash hidden on the outside.'

He paused and she sensed he was having a little difficulty keeping his voice level.

'He spread the word that the money was up for grabs to anyone who could get him free.'

She snapped her head up. 'You don't mean someone has actually—?'

'Yeah. Someone busted Brazos McGraw out a few weeks ago. The authorities tried to keep it quiet but news like that is hard to suppress and the word's spreading. I've made a few contacts on the wrong side of the law during my own chores and I *talked* to a couple, picked up a lead.'

There was a whole lot left unspoken there, she guessed.

'You're sure that Brazos McGraw is coming here?'

'Yeah. To use the Shuffle. He made a deal.'

He paused and she stiffened even more. 'You— I don't want to hear this but, I think I must! My father. . . ?'

'I dunno. No! Really, I don't know. Not for sure, anyway, but there *was* a deal made with someone. McGraw's loot in return for safe passage up into the undeveloped territories, maybe even Canada.'

She remained silent, staring at him unwaveringly.

'That's what I found out through my own contacts.'

'No doubt with fists and guns!'

He narrowed his eyes at her tone. 'I was dealing with tough men – *mighty* tough men. And every one of them scared white at the thought of McGraw finding out they might've helped the law close in on him.'

'Was my father one of those men?'

'I told you, I never found out for sure, but – well, he'd seen a lot of men through that Pipeline. I guess he'd have been approached, at least.'

'But he would never help a monster like McGraw! He just *wouldn't*!'

'Well, like I said, I never learned those details. It was enough that we had word that Brazos was making use of the Shuffle, so I came here.'

'You came here? You weren't *sent* here?'

He said nothing for a moment, his face unchanging, then he nodded jerkily. All right. Officially, I'm a rogue marshal, but there won't be any *real* effort to rope me in and clip my wings, not until *after* Brazos is dealt with, if you know what I mean.'

'I do. And I understand how your superiors would take advantage of your actions with someone as vile as Brazos McGraw ... even if they felt obliged to chastise you afterward— What're you smiling at?'

'Your choice of words: "chastise"? Judas Priest, they'd throw *me* into jail if they figured they had to, to quieten things down.'

'My God! You must have a formidable reputation! No wonder my father was leery of you when you showed up here.'

'I'm not here to smear your father's name, Margaret. I'm here to kill Brazos because he murdered my wife, and I'll do whatever's necessary to get it done.'

'And if my father's name should come up?'

He said nothing and the long stare continued, unwaveringly, until, finally, she looked away.

'My God. I wish you'd never come into my life.'

'That would be something I think I'd regret.'

He rose suddenly and when she looked up from staring down into her lap where she was clenching her hands, he was gone – somewhere out into the night.

She half-rose, then dropped back into the chair, took one long, deep, shuddering breath and covered her face with her hands.

The thing about Brazos McGraw was that he didn't *look* like the monster he really was.

Somewhere in his early thirties, he appeared years younger and he had a pleasant enough face and a charming smile – which far too many people had been taken in by, to their regret.

Even robbing a bank or a Wells Fargo Depot he was likely to share a smoke with the man he was holding at gunpoint, chatting away in friendly manner. Then, on the last draw on his smoke, he would bring up his gun and shoot them.

Not always fatally: if he could spare the time he would wait and watch them in their death throes. If time was short, more often than not he would snap a vesta into flame, plunge the burning head into a boxful of matches and toss the flaring mess on to the wounded man – or woman. . . .

He seemed satisfied to ride away with their dying screams ringing in his ears.

He was smart enough never to leave witnesses, which was probably why he wasn't sentenced to hang when he was caught. It was said that his defending lawyer retired immediately after the verdict and lived a very pleasant life, able to pick and choose any work that came his way.

And even that amount of money left plenty more for Brazos to get the word out that he could pay – *handsomely* – anyone who went to the trouble of getting him out of the Comstock Penitentiary.

Somebody had finally managed it and that suited Mitchell Slade to a 'T'.

He knew he could never reach McGraw in the high-security prison, but once the man was out then he was fair game.

It had taken a deal of persuasion to convince his

boss, the figurehead official Federal Marshal – a political appointment – that McGraw would make for Hatfield. The Service had been watching the place with all the rumours that spread about some mysterious 'Pipeline' to freedom, mostly known simply as the Shuffle.

But, in the end, due to his past success in his job as a deputy marshal, Slade had been assigned to track down the rumours to their source, starting with persistent talk about the sheriff, Lew Towney, making deals with desperate men on the run and steering them to the escape route.

There had been talk about its existence for a long time but nothing could be proved until Lew Towney made one of his deals on such a scale that it simply had to be officially investigated. And it would need a mighty tough and dedicated man to do it. . . .

Coming at about the same time as Brazos McGraw made his successful prison break, the obvious man to assign to the job was Mitchell Slade – the most dedicated and gun-swift of all the lawmen – and the one with the biggest stake in apprehending McGraw.

The Chief Marshal knew he would not be disappointed unless – *unless* McGraw somehow managed to kill Slade first.

And that would be the *only* way to stop him.

But the chief figured that McGraw, tough as he was supposed to be, had only just managed to survive his brutal time in the penitentiary. If he showed any sense, once he was free, he would put as much distance as he could between *any* kind of law and himself.

He was wrong.

Brazos McGraw was not dumb – certainly not the craven fool he had seemed to be when his well-rehearsed performance had tricked the guards long enough to give his waiting rescuer the chance he needed to effect his escape.

Then, when he learned that the man assigned to hunt him down was none other than Mitchell Slade, who had – long ago – sworn to kill Brazos because he had murdered his family, he knew there could be only one way for real escape.

When Slade was dead.

The simple answer to that was, of course: *make sure – damned sure –* he *was*!

And as soon as possible.

CHAPTER 10

THE WAITING GAME

Marshal Mitchell Slade knew it was going to be a waiting game. He was impatient but he could fight that – *if he had to* – and he did. No other way. Brazos was in control of whatever was to happen now.

And Brazos had plenty of patience: he could get through just about anything simply with 'anticipation', looking forward to whatever evil his mind could conjure up – and there was *plenty* of it! – until the moment when he could unleash his sadism.

Slade had only come face to face with him once: alvost three years ago. By something close to pure luck, he had cornered McGraw, climbed on top of a rock and looked down into the man's camp.

'End of the trail, Brazos,' he'd said coldly and raised his six-gun even as McGraw spun so fast he was little more than a blur as he whipped out his Colt. Slade had ducked instinctively. Then there was a clatter near his head, a few sparks from the rock and something heavy thudded against his hat, knocking it off even as he stumbled to one knee.

He dropped his own six-gun, groped for it as blood spilled into one eye, half-blinding him. His hand closed over the weapon and he brought it up, feeling the elation as he thumbed back the hammer, lined up the sight on McGraw as he ran for cover and . . . the hammer *clunked* on an empty chamber.

Not possible! He knew he had just filled all six chambers in the cylinder and . . . *a misfire! God, not now!*

It was no misfire, it was as it seemed: the hammer had fallen on an empty chamber!

The thoughts flashed through his mind and, glancing down as Brazos laughed from the bushes where he had disappeared, Slade cursed and flung the useless gun away.

It had been Brazos's own gun! He must've flung it at the marshal when he ran out of bullets. It hit him in the head, so that when he stumbled, vision blurred and ears ringing, he had dropped his own gun. And had picked up Brazos McGraw's empty Colt by mistake – *a mistake that could've cost him his life.*

Groping now, Slade found his own dropped Colt and gave chase but McGraw had already climbed a small cliff where he'd had a second getaway mount waiting at the top.

He slid the rifle out of the saddle scabbard and shot the lawman as he ran towards the cliff face.

103

Slade went down hard, hit somewhere high in the chest, he figured, and lay there in the dust, dazed, consciousness coming and going, as he tried to crawl behind a rock, tasting blood in the back of his throat.

'Aw, shucks, Mitch!' McGraw's voice reached him through the buzzing pain: he was on the verge of passing out. 'How's that for luck? My last rifle bullet. Man, I won't forget this, I kid you not, you bastard! You ought to be *dead*, but I can wait, I got plenty time, more than you think, an' when we meet again— Aw, hell, you know what'll happen. But here's a thought or two for you to keep you warm nights: I *liked* your wife. *Mmm-my! Yes!* Lovely smile – right up to the time I snapped her neck!'

Then that maniacal laugh that would stay with Slade until the day he died. . . .

'I'll be seein' you, Mitch! Sleep well.'

And then he was gone.

Now, it was three years later and Marshal Mitchell Slade found himself shaking, not from any crack on his head from an empty gun, but from that terrible memory.

Well, he'd waited all this time, he could wait a little longer to get his hands on the murdering swine.

And afterward? A question he had asked himself often.

'Who cared?' he said aloud. 'Who the hell cared what happened then. . . ?'

Now, he was holed up in Sheriff Towney's old office in Hatfield. It was near the north edge of town: Slade

104

had a hunch that if Brazos came in – and he would have to sooner or later to make sure the Pipeline was ready and operating as it should – it would be from this direction.

He checked his rifle and Colt, by feel, in the darkness of the office, glanced up in time to see a small but bright flash out there in the night, a flash with a faint bluish tinge to it. He knew what that meant!

Light reflecting from a lens. Like field-glasses or a rifle's telescopic sight.

He dropped flat at the thought and a moment later the window above his head exploded, showering him with broken glass.

Without hesitation, he leapt to his feet, held the rifle across his body and as high as his face, then launched himself at the office door. He hit it hard enough to tear it off its hinges and it fell with a clatter on the landing even as he skidded, rolled off and twisted, to come up crouching in the gutter.

It was pure luck that he glimpsed the flash again. His Winchester came to his shoulder and he triggered and levered three fast shots in the direction of that flash and was up and running towards it before the echoes had died.

That damn chest wound from three years earlier slowed him down some, though. Fact, it had done too many times over the intervening years.

It turned out he had been *mighty* lucky, because the bullet had nicked the top of one lung, just deep enough to destroy, in part, a couple of the airways. They'd healed, but come winters he always had the

105

wheezes – congestion that couldn't get past the damaged area. Cut his breath to a series of screeching gasps at times, specially when running, and he hàd to admit it was getting slowly worse as he grew older.

Well, pretty soon he aimed to come face to face with Brazos McGraw and he might not have to worry about breathing at all. *The hell with thinking like that!* He aimed to walk away from that meeting and leave Brazos for the buzzards.

What happened to him didn't – *wouldn't* – matter a damn.

He scrubbed a hand down his face, breathing through his teeth. Then some instinct made him dive to the left just as a rifle fired two fast shots that fanned past his face. Thrown off by their closeness, his answering shot went wild.

But he had the dry-gulcher's position now, or where he had been before he fired, now the man had decided to run!

The crashing of the brush was easy to follow and he heard him fall, giving Slade a chance to gain four or five yards. He saw the bushwhacker's blurred outline against the pale earth of some sort of natural wall.

Slade dropped to one knee, brought up the Winchester and fired two fast shots. His target yelled as the bullets kicked gravel into his face and, gagging and grunting, he slid back to the ground.

And when he looked up, the tall marshal was standing above him, his smoking rifle barrel pressing into the killer's breastbone. The man put shaky hands up in front of his face.

'Don't! G-gimme a . . . break, Slade!'

It was Red Connor.

'How about I make it as good a break as the one you were about to give me, Red?'

'No – don't! I got a wife an' . . . kids!'

'I did, too – once,' Slade gritted. 'Until Brazos McGraw got to 'em.'

'Aw, listen, Slade! I-I don't go in for killin' women an' kids! I'm broke! I need some money bad—'

'I'll go along with that – but we both know the real reason, don't we?'

Red frowned. 'I-I dunno what you're—'

Slade made a growling sound, clipped the man across the head with the rifle butt. Red grunted and dropped to his knees. 'Red, you're just no damn good, any way you look at it. You've been on the edge of the law for years – you and your sidekick, "Big" Jock! There was a helluva lot of bad in that little son of a bitch.'

'He was my pard!' Red suddenly snarled; any pretence he had been using to make Slade think he was just being used by Brazos was now gone. 'You killed him! No hesitation, just drew an' – an' nailed him dead centre!'

'You should've made your try at the same time and I'd've mebbe got you too.'

Red Connor couldn't hold back any longer. He growled deep in his throat and, in a brave but stupid action, launched himself at the marshal, who still

107

held his rifle.

Slade hadn't been expecting it: afterwards he figured he had underestimated just how close Red Connor and Big Jock had been.

But Red had risked his life now and his hand slapped Slade's gunhand aside as he rammed his head into the lawman's midriff. Mitchell Slade went down to one knee, toppled sideways as Connor's work boots thudded into his ribs. One caught the edge of his left hip so that when he tried to push up, the leg collapsed under him.

Red shouted in elation, lashed out with his right boot: it would have taken Slade's head off if it had landed. But the marshal was functioning properly now and he stepped nimbly to one side and Connor staggered . . . right into the whizzing uppercut Slade launched. It cracked against the side of Connor's jaw and he stumbled. Slade strode after him, hooking one of Connor's legs out from under him with a brutal sideways kick. Red crashed to the ground.

He was an experienced fighter in the rough and tumble of the frontier and he somersaulted, not away from Slade, but towards him.

It was quite acrobatic, a true somersault, so that his legs flailed over and he put all his weight behind them, driving bootheels into Slade's lower body.

The marshal went down to one knee and Red was sure he had him now, bared his teeth in a victory grin and stepped in, right fist drawn way back so as to inflict as much damage as possible.

It would have been considerable, but Mitchell

Slade hadn't served for years as one of the most successful federal marshals ever by standing still to have his face punched to the back of his head.

He not only ducked, he dropped flat, and Connor's impetus carried him forward swiftly – off-balance. His arms flailed wildly as he fought to regain control of his fall but it was too late.

Marshal Slade set his feet, moved his hips slightly so he was set firmly, and rammed his fists left-right-left-right into Red's midriff. The man gagged sickly, doubled up.

Slade's knee lifted into the contorted face, sending Connor flailing backward several paces before he tripped over a deadfall and stretched out – unconscious.

The lawman was glad to drop on to a nearby rock and let his head hang as he gasped for breath, feeling the tightness in his chest. It made him cough, violently and long, and he was mighty glad Red was out of things for now.

He took down his saddle canteen and swilled the blood-taste from his mouth, scooped a handful of icy water over his bleeding, puffy face. He badly wanted a cigarette but figured it would be stupid when his breathing was already so short and laboured.

So he waited, seated on his boulder, chest heaving.

It seemed a long, long time before Red Connor groaned sickly and began to struggle back to consciousness.

'Hope Brazos paid you well, Red,' Slade said, his voice startling the groggy dry-gulcher. 'There ain't a judge this side of Canada who won't give you at least seven years . . . more likely ten . . . for trying to kill a lawman going about his duty. Or, he could hang you. Bet Brazos never reminded you of that when he got you to set me up.'

'What the hell you know!' Red spat some blood. 'I told him I'd do it for nothin' 'cause you killed Big Jock!'

'Thought you said you did it for the money?'

'Aw – well, to hell with it! It ain't any of your business!'

Connor sat there, moaning how sick he felt until Slade kicked him in the ribs . . . a blow hard enough to knock the wind out of the dry-gulcher so that he fell on to his side. He looked up fearfully with wide eyes.

'You know what I'm waiting to hear, Red.'

'Go to hell!'

'I guess we could meet up there some time, but right now, tell . . . me . . . about . . . Brazos.' He paused and gave the battered man a glimpse of his six-gun coming up.

'Hey, wait!' Red yelled frantically. 'Judas Priest! You – you can't just kill a man like that!'

'You were just gonna kill me. I can do the same to you, because I wear a badge, nothing will happen to me. But you—'

'Hell, Marshal! He'll shoot me where I stand!'

'If you're stupid enough to hang around – could be. But if you *don't* tell me, you can start thinking about being with the big boys in the State Pen. Judge might give you ten years, maybe only five, but won't matter: you won't last a week with them hard-timers. *Depraved*, someone described 'em.'

Red squirmed and moaned on the ground, then said in a rush, 'Brazos picked me up at Drawstring Creek when I was – well, I was sort of brandin' some cows.'

'With a running iron. Yeah, well, never mind that!'

'He took me high up that razorback peak to a kinda big niche in the wall above the hairpin bend in the crick. There's a small cave I never knew was there an'— OK! *OK*! He told me he wanted me to-to shoot you. He knew you were in Lew Towney's office. Told me he'd been watchin' a long time an' he was gonna pick you off before he went up the Shuffle. Then he offered to pay me to do it, 'cause he knew I wanted your guts for killin' Big Jock.'

Slade nodded slowly. Brazos's brain might be kinked into sadism, but there was nothing wrong with his deductions.

'You reckon he's still out there on the razorback?'

'We-ll – he was when he turned me loose.'

'He could be miles away by now, or, maybe, even watching us right this minute . . . see if you did your job.'

Red's legs wobbled with sudden weakness – and Slade decided he might just have guessed right! It was the kind of thing Brazos would do: set up the fool he'd hired to take a potshot at Slade and wait in the wings for the result.

Which meant he could be in Brazos's sights – right *now*!

As he hit the ground he heard a rifle crack from upslope, then a grunt close by and the thud of Red Connor's body falling. The second shot almost hit the marshal as he lunged aside. The bullet tugged at a loose section of his shirt and then he was throwing himself under some brush, kicking, raising a cloud of twigs and dead leaves and dust as he ploughed on deeper into the bushes.

His wide shoulders jammed him up briefly and two more bullets went mighty close, followed by that unmistakable laugh of Brazos McGraw.

'That damn Red! Left it too late. Can't see proper now to finish it, but *I'll be ba-ack*!'

The killer sing-songed the last, laughed again and then there was silence. Straining his ears as hard as he could, Mitchell Slade still did not hear Brazos quit the mountain.

But as the man had said: he'd be back.

And he'd find Slade waiting – *or would he*!

Mitchell Slade had suddenly decided that he had waited long enough.

It was time to go out and drive Brazos McGraw into the ground – preferably with half-a-dozen bullets from Slade's rifle in him.

Brazos had shot Red dead centre which told Slade that the killer hadn't lost any of his shooting prowess in the intervening years in the penitentiary.

Nor his ruthlessness.

By the same token, Marshal Mitchell Slade had lost absolutely *none* of the churning hate that drove him on and on and on. . . .

112

Nor would he.

Unless one of Brazos's bullets stopped him.

Not much of a God-fearing man, Mitchell Slade lifted his drawn face slightly and looked up to the stars – no moon yet. He hesitated, started to speak very softly.

'Lord, if You're out there somewhere, just let me destroy Brazos McGraw. Then You can have my soul and send it straight to Hell – I don't want no other deal!'

A half-hour later, he thought his prayer had been answered.

He found the hiding place Red Connor had described on the razorback: *right above the hairpin bend in Drawstring Creek. . . .*

Even with only the starlight to guide him, Slade could make out a black shadow that must mark the entrance Red had spoken of: a kind of 'fold' in the rockface.

It would be a tough climb in the dark, and his breathing was already coming hard as he started making his way up, rifle thrust through the back of his gunbelt, barrel down. The butt rapped him on the head each time he heaved up another foot or so, but – *no choice!* He *had* to check out that cave, even if he thought Brazos was still up there waiting.

But it was all a wasted effort, and if he'd had enough breath to spare he would have cussed till sun-up. Not that that would have done him any good . . . only released some of the pent-up tension that had filled his big frame.

He put his back against a smooth part of the wall and slid down to a sitting position.

His heart was hammering and he had to face the fact he had wasted a good deal of energy he couldn't really afford just to gain nothing.

Now he had to climb back down – or learn to fly.

Gathering himself for the return, he stopped dead in his thoughts: *but was it for nothing?* Sure it was, for him, but it was too easy, the way he'd found this place. And Brazos should have been waiting to pick him off.

No. Maybe not!

The way the killer thought, he could have *wanted* Slade to find the place and waste time looking around for tracks and—

Well, there *were* tracks, hard to see in the gloom. He wanted to ignore them now, but he couldn't afford to pass up the chance that maybe – *just maybe* – he was wrong and Brazos had grown careless. But it would be mighty chancy to strike a vesta to see just where those tracks led. He turned and lunged for the entrance, having to skid to a stop to keep from tumbling over the steep ledge. He was going to have to reverse his climb now, and going down would be slower, more of a strain.

'Hey, Marshal!'

Slade froze as that dreaded voice boomed around the razorback. There were so many echoes he couldn't tell exactly from where it originated. But he didn't have to wait long to find out.

Brazos McGraw appeared out of some rocks below

– a shadowy figure, forking the marshal's own horse!

'Nice mount, Slade. I like him, so think I'll keep him. Was gonna leave you mine but – well, mebbe you need the exercise, huh? Know what I mean? So I drove my hoss off an' he fell over a cliff. Wonder you didn't hear him holler!'

Marshal Slade's insides were frozen. He had this sudden, belly-wrenching hunch because he knew McGraw's background all too well.

The man was making sure he was going to be afoot!

'Aw, it don't take you this long to figure it out, Slade!' Brazos called again, an edge of sly confidence in his words. 'You know I'm gonna be back in Hatfield while you're still tryin' to find your way out of these hills *on foot, remember*!'

Slade dropped to one knee but before he had the rifle to his shoulder, searching for a clear shot at Brazos, the man had disappeared into the deep shadows of the huge boulders. His hated, maniacal laugh that Slade recalled from three years ago rang around the rocks.

'You know why I wanna go back to Hatfield, huh?' The words came hard on the crazy laughter – put on and exaggerated, Slade knew, but it still didn't stop the griping pain that twisted his belly. 'Sure you do. You're dumb, but not *that* dumb!'

'Goddamn you, Brazos!' The marshal's voice cracked as a cold fear gripped his heart. 'You got no call to do it!'

'Wrong, you bastard! I took your wife 'cause I felt like it and it got you riled enough to run me down

115

and put me in that stinkin' Pen! I got out an' now I've come back for you! I hear you got a nifty li'l cookie back in Hatfield and that sounds pretty good to me. Ain't a blonde like your wife was, but hell, hair colour don't matter that much, not if they's all woman underneath! Just a nice, warm woman's body. . . .'

A ringing silence.

'Huh? What was that you said, Slade ol' pard. . . ? Can't hear yooooou! But bet you know just what I'm thinkin' – *and you're right,* you son of a bitch! 'Course, I'll be long gone by the time you walk to a ranch where you can borrow a hoss, so take it easy! She'll be there when you get back to Hatfield – *you can count on that*!'

He started to ride away, ducked back when Slade fired two shots at him, the bullets ricocheting from the rocks protecting him.

'Hell! *Must*'ve rattled you, wastin' your lead like that! Good to know I can do it. But you ain't seen nothin' yet. Just wait'll you find dear l'il Margaret – or what I leave of her!'

Slade choked on any sort of reply, stupidly emptying the magazine after the killer he could no longer see because of the intervening rocks.

Brazos didn't even bother laughing this time.

CHAPTER 11

EMPTY GUNS

The climb had been bad enough and the descent not much better, hanging by his fingertips, scraping knees and elbows, even his face, as he clung to the cliff like a fly on a wall.

He dropped the last six feet – he thought – but his estimate was wrong in this faint light and he hit sooner than expected, his knees lifting up and almost breaking his nose. He spat blood, mopped his nostrils and mouth and deliberately stood very still, making himself breathe deeply and slowly through his mouth. It hurt some to take a deep breath, because his exertions were overworking the damaged section of lung. But it helped clear the dizziness, and when he felt steady again, he got to his feet, used his empty rifle like a walking stick until feeling came back into his numbed legs.

By then his mind had washed away the building panic and he slowed down, took a quick assessment of his position – and *condition* – while he cleared the rifle barrel of dirt.

Brazos had outwitted him! He had to admit it.

Nothing could stop the killer from getting to Margaret now. Without a horse, Slade would drag behind for hours, and, during that time— Don't think about it!

He didn't have to put it into words: he had a headful of disturbing images that brought a tremble to his hands and an icy knot to the pit of his stomach.

The fact was, he simply could not believe it was all happening again – just like Brazos going after Angie and—

But this time it was worse, because *he* had totally failed to foresee Brazos McGraw's intentions.

And – *Margaret*! He hadn't admitted it to himself before, but he did now: she was the first woman he had felt anything for since Angie had died at McGraw's cruel hands, and now, because of his failure to acknowledge this, he had put her at very great risk.

The certain knowledge that McGraw would kill her in any one of his sadistic ways – *maybe more than one*! – almost shut down his mind.

While all these shocking admissions had – *finally* – shaken him into action, he knew he'd still fumbled it badly.

Too eager for the capture; too slow to openly

admit that Brazos's twisted mind could – and would – outsmart him—

And now look at the mess he was in.

'To hell with *you*, pard! You're used to risking your own hide and having it banged up, but someone like Margaret Towney wasn't meant to fall into the hands of a maniac like Brazos McGraw! No more than Angie was. . . .'

Margaret's the one who's going to suffer and you're the only one who can do anything about it.

The only one.

'A mighty comforting thought!' he gritted bitterly.

But, inevitably, other thoughts followed: the first being, what could he do about it?

And the answer was still the same: *nothing that he could think of.*

It hit home even harder when he heard a horse galloping up along the high ridge that led to the trail back to Hatfield. There would be only one rider up there at this time.

He suddenly became acutely aware of his own aching legs and the increasing pain in his feet as they swelled in his boots from all the climbing and walking.

Well, he'd known all along he would never make it in time, not on foot. Hell! Even his guns were empty! Sure, at a pinch, he could maybe rake up two or three cartridges, but that wouldn't be enough! Nowhere *near* enough. Then—

'Red Connor!'

He said the name aloud, head coming up and searching the dark area where he knew Red's body to be. Red had been still wearing his gunbelt when Brazos had shot him down and left the body where it fell.

And he wondered where Red had left his horse!

He'd have stashed it someplace well away from where he lay in ambush, waiting to get a shot at Slade through the side window of the dead sheriff's office. *But not too far!*

Now what the hell was up there in reasonable distance of where Red had set up his ambush. . . ?

He thought hard and fast, then forced himself to slow down. It was a long time since he had been in this country until lately. There was the ledge where Red had tried to kill him – it was just a protrusion of rock, hanging out over the edge of a drop. But nothing down there – anyway, if he'd left the horse below, Slade would have seen it, or would have sensed the marshal's mount and likely whinnied.

But, *behind* that ledge where Red had waited, aiming at the Law Office with Slade inside, was—

'Granny's Ear!' A short tangle of gulches that ran off the draw, ending in a bushy oval with an egg-shaped patch of grass in the middle – enough sweet mountain grass to ensure it would keep a horse munching to fill its belly, rather than whistling up any other mount it heard to come and share.

He was running already, stumbled twice, grazed his hands when he put them down as he rolled, but came up with legs working again. In minutes, after two more falls because of over-eager running, he found Red's body, ripped off the gunbelt. There was no six-gun but that didn't matter: Brazos may've taken it, or Red might've lost— *The hell with it!*

Slade had his own Colt, and his rifle, both the same calibre – .44 – though the short revolver cartridge did not shoot all that well from a long gun. *But it'd be good enough!*

He was armed again, and if he could find Red Connor's mount where he hoped it would be—

'Judas!' he spat bitterly, savagely thrusting brush aside, looking at the tip of the rising moon behind the ridge now. 'I'll still never make it in time to cut off Brazos before he gets to Margaret. But, by God, I'll be breathing down his neck before he can afford the time to stop and do whatever he's planning!'

That part he didn't want to think about as he groped his way through the first of the tangles that led to Granny's Ear. If he was wrong, he didn't even know what he could try next.

Then he grinned: he had heard the stomp and quizzical snorting of a horse back there, probably still feeding in the egg-shaped patch of grass. His heart hammered, and he bared his teeth as he finally saw the animal: a grey mare, with a splash of white beneath its left eye.

And still saddled!

It looked right back at him and whinnied.

'*Brazos, you snake – I'm coming to get you!*'

He punched in the crown of his hat and poured in

121

some water from the saddle canteen. He shook the container while the horse drank and figured it was still about half full. He swallowed a couple of mouthfuls.

Both Colt and rifle were loaded now: he had taken off his own empty cartridge belt, strapped on Red's, having to adjust the belt only a little. But he found he had to lengthen the stirrups on the saddle because he had much longer legs than Red.

The horse was co-operative and Slade wasted no time mounting and riding it out of the convoluted draws of Granny's Ear.

Once into open country again, he turned the horse towards town.

That was when his belly gave a lurch: it would be all guesswork from here on in!

He *had* to assume Margaret was at her place, or, at least, still in town. He didn't know where else she might go. He glanced at the pale sky in the east.

The rising sun outlined the range, the moon only a pale cut-out now in a gap between the glowing, crimson clouds, sliding inevitably towards the west.

But this was on his side of the range – the town was on the far side and would already have had sunlight for at least a half-hour, maybe longer.

So Margaret could be up and about.

And what difference would that make? None – except to make it easier for Brazos to get to her.

The grey protested with a high whinny and a jerky weaving of its rump as he rammed home his spurs to urge it to greater speed.

*

It was early, but Margaret Towney had been rising early for years.

A hangover from the days when the family had a small ranch and it had been her job, when young, to feed the hens and keep the crowing roosters quiet, exercise the horses kept for everyday mounts, clean out the barn and check the water pump and – well, the hundred-and-one other apparently minor but essential chores that involved farming or small-time ranching.

She had liked it – still did. She enjoyed the freshness of early morning, watching the sun show gradually over the range, seeing the golden light flood the slopes like spilled paint . . . chasing the shadows, or making some of its own and—

Suddenly, he was there!

She gasped, for she hadn't heard him or had any inkling he was within ten miles of the place.

Now, Brazos McGraw nodded pleasantly and gave her an easy smile as he stood there, hipshot, those disturbing eyes narrowed, roving her body like – spiders. *Making her flesh crawl but she tried not to show that.*

'Nice time of day, ain't it? I used to do the early-mornin' chores on our farm outside Deadwood. Din' like it at first: the old man kinda had it in for me, made me work daylight till dark . . . figured if he tired me out, I wouldn't get into so much trouble. . . .'

123

The smile faded or at least tightened around the edges and he nodded, but as if he was only confirming something to himself, rather than for Margaret's benefit.

'He was my father but we never did get along any too well. Ma died in a fire and, later, he married again, some woman who already had a daughter.' He shook his head jerkily. 'She was buck-toothed but otherwise not bad – no, not bad at all. . . .' His voice went a little dreamy with rememberance and then his narrow face seemed to tighten up. 'Man! The hell he created when he found me with her in the barn one sun-up. It'd've been all right if she hadn't screamed so damn loud.'

Margaret was tense, unmoving as a statue, watching his face as he recalled an unpleasant incident from his past.

'Ye-aah! Old bastard whipped the hide offa my back. You wanna see it? I still got the scars an' – no? Well, don't blame you – it ain't pretty. But I watched that cane he was beltin' me with, seen the blood flyin', spottin' the woodshed wall, and suddenly I realized it was *my* blood. *Bastard!* He was enjoyin' himself. Till I took the pickaxe and pinned him to the wall with it! *Huh!* That stopped the son of a bitch— *Hey!* Don't run off! I ain't finished yet!'

He lunged at the girl as she turned and started to sprint away. He caught up in a few strides, yanked her roughly to him and looked down into her contorted face.

'He was a hard sonuver – bossin' me 'round like

124

some damn slave. Ah! Miserable bastard deserved to die! Too bad it was so quick!'

'But, your own father!'

'I spit on his memory! Hell, I never had much choice, did I? *Did I?*'

He roared this last and it made her wince and jump. He shook her roughly and she struggled to free herself, but he was too strong, held her without seeming to exert himself.

'Hey! You are a *looker*, ain't you? Smell nice, too. Slade's wife, Angie, she smelled nice. L'il bit different to you but real nice. Kinda got me goin'.' He suddenly leered, shaking her again. 'Y'know what I mean?'

She did.

And she froze, then almost instantly gathered a scream, even though she knew it wouldn't do much good out here. The rest of the street was sleeping – no, even that wasn't right: the other couple of houses were empty; the town was slowly dying and folk were moving out every week and—

He felt her chest beginning to swell as she made ready to scream and, just as she opened her mouth, he jabbed her violently in the midriff with three stiffened fingers.

Margaret gagged and her knees gave way and he let her fall. She leaned forward, gasping and wheezing, and he twisted his hands in her long black hair that had come loose from the bandanna that had held it close to her head but was now falling half across her face.

She heard his breath hiss in sharply between his teeth.

'Oh, *my*! Now *that* is somethin' that *really* gets me goin'! Hair fallin' across a woman's face! Awwwww! Come on, sweetmeat! There's a patch of grass under yonder tree an' I'm randy as a stallion!'

'I can change that!' Her voice trembled as she spoke and his grin widened, until—

She twisted as he reached for the top of her blouse, and brought up a knee savagely into his crotch.

He dropped with a sickening, choking scream, clawed the air where she'd been a moment ago and, through a red haze of increasing pain, saw her trying to grab his gun.

He was suffering, but raw instinct made him clamp his hands tight on the gun and then he struck at her, the barrel catching her above the right eye, splitting the skin. She staggered and it took him off-guard so that he stumbled. She stomped on his instep and he howled, went halfway down to the ground, one hand supporting his twisted body. His mouth was hanging open, making a rasping sound as pain knotted him.

Then she was running for the street, head throbbing.

He was down in the dust now, curled up, knees drawn high into his chest, rocking back and forth in an effort to ease his suffering.

He fumbled at his six-gun again, swore as he dropped it. But, as he was lying on his side, it only fell a few inches. He clawed it out of the dust and cocked the hammer even as he brought it up into line with her running figure, his hand shaking so that he had to use his other hand to steady his gun arm.

He triggered impatiently but at the same moment, Margaret's flying feet turned on a rocky patch and she cried out as she sprawled. She banged her head hard, felt the warmth of fresh blood snaking down her face.

It must have looked to Brazos as if his bullet had hit her and knocked her off her feet.

The world spun out of focus for her and one hand closed around a smooth stone. Just before blackness closed in, she heard him stumbling towards her, muttering.

Words she didn't want to hear!

'Din' mean to hurt you bad, sweetmeat, but it won't make no difference, see? *No difference at all* Come here! An' let's have some fun!'

The sound of the gunshot had stopped Marshal Mitchell Slade in his tracks.

He knew what it meant and his guts clamped solid.

Margaret must have made a run for it and by this time Brazos would use any means at all to stop her.

Including shooting her down coldly.

He saw them then, just clear of the end of the street, on the slope leading up to the patch of desert that swung close to town here.

He froze when he saw her sprawling, Those damn gunshots!

It looked as if at least one had found its target.

He had been leading Red Connor's mount but swung up into the saddle now and set it running down the street.

The clatter of hoofs brought Brazos swinging around in his saddle. Even from here, Slade could see him give a start. Obviously he hadn't expected to find the marshal so close *and mounted*!

Then Brazos lifted his rifle as he kneed his mount around and Slade threw himself from the saddle. But Brazos wasn't shooting at him: he shot the horse and Slade didn't manage to clear the saddle in time.

He went down with the animal and had his hands full fighting to keep his legs clear. He almost made it, but his left boot was caught by the falling animal and it writhed and kicked and whinnied, pinning him by that leg. For some minutes Mitchell Slade thought he was either going to get his head kicked in or have his ankle crushed.

But luck hadn't entirely deserted him.

His boot was over a small depression in the ground and there was a layer of coarse sand in the bottom, washed there by rains in the past. It gave him partial cushioning but while the ankle wasn't crushed it was rolled back and forth with the dying horse's convulsions. He'd had more pleasant experiences though no bones broke.

Thankful for small mercies, he writhed in behind the now quivering bulk of the mount as it gradually expired from Brazos's bullets. Another slug thudded into the grey horse and Slade huddled closer, keeping his head down.

'Hell! I'm tempted to finish the job, Slade!' The lawman heard the rifle lever clash as Brazos jacked another cartridge into the breech. 'But you caught me in a good mood!'

He laughed coldly. 'How about that? I can see you're kinda stuck there – could even work your way out in a while. Sooooo, tell you what I'm gonna do.' He turned and shook the sagging girl roughly. 'Me and your galfriend are just gonna head out across the desert. The State Line's on that side an' I'll cross it when I'm good 'n' ready. What I want you to see is me an Sweetie here makin' our way so far ahead you'll never catch up. Nah, that ain't right! I *want* you to catch up eventually so you can see what I've done to her in the meantime. Oh, don't worry! She'll still be alive – well, kinda, but likely she'll be wishin' she was dead and mebbe I'll oblige so you can watch. I'll decide later. Right now we gotta get goin' so we can get down and smooch a little. Did I say a "*little*"? No matter. You know what I mean. For now, *adios!*'

'*Mitch!*' Margaret's cry was plaintive and he saw the blood on her face and thought it was from a bullet wound, a scalp crease, maybe—

'Margaret! I'll. . . .'

He never finished the sentence.

Brazos fired three fast shots that forced Slade to duck and when he untangled himself from the dead mount's legs, the killer and Margaret were disappearing over the first rise.

He flopped back: he didn't know what good it

129

would do, but he thought he might as well take stock of his present situation. For, right now, he couldn't see any way that it was going to improve.

CHAPTER 12

PURSUIT AND PROBLEMS

He forced himself to sit on the dead horse and try to work things out.

The most obvious was that Brazos had a mount and he and the girl could be across the desert before Slade could travel more than a mile or two – if that – on foot.

Grim as the fact was, he had no intention of giving up. How could he? Margaret was out there – well ahead, but *there*, and if *he* did nothing to help her, who would?

It was gut-wrenching to ask such a question in his present state of mind but it had to be faced. The worst thing about it was there was no comforting answer.

Hell, he would need a damn good mount to catch

up, anyway, but just get him within rifle shot and he'd pick off Brazos like a bottle swinging on a string.

He was a good shot *but a hell of a lot of good that did*, right now, even knowing it was true.

It still came back to getting within shooting range.

And it had to be before Brazos went entirely loco.

No need to spell it out: it was knowledge that could not only horrify him to the point of inaction, but also be used to drive him on, to keep him in pursuit – no matter what.

He had a little tobacco left, took out his sack and papers and rolled a thin cigarette. It tasted like old boots but just the drawing in of the smoke and letting it fill his lungs, drift out of his nostrils, gave some sort of satisfaction. Damned if he knew how or why but it did calm him some.

And he needed to *stay* calm. In fact, it began to bother him that he might not stay calm: in a weak moment he might give way and charge out there like a madman and to hell with the consequences, just to be doing something.

'*Come on!* You know better than that, for Chris'sakes!'

It was as if all his years of being a lawman, and a mighty tough *hombre* before that in several different fields, had never happened. Only once before had he felt so helpless and plain damned *scared* and *that* was when this same Brazos McGraw, a mongrel masquerading as a human being, had abducted Angie and—

No need to put *that* into words, not even *silent*

words: as long as he lived he would never forget the anguish and utter helplessness he had felt.

'OK!' he gritted aloud. 'OK, I can't let it happen again! And I won't! Now, *that's* it! Take everything from that point and *move forward* – literally!'

He was on his feet, checking his guns without realizing it, his ribcage thudding in time to his accelerated heartbeat.

'Good Lord Almighty! I-I hate this frustration so I *have to do something about it.*'

Basically, it seemed impossible.

He adjusted his scuffed old field-glasses and—

There they were! A long way off, and Brazos had the girl draped across the saddle in front of him.

Hell! Was she even moving? Hard to tell from this distance and with such small glasses.

He felt like he was choking and he recognized the edge of panic, like that first time in battle at Antietam – the bullets flying, cold steel flashing, slicing through.

He tried to roll one last cigarette – there was probably just enough tobacco – but his hands were too clumsy.

Strangely, the failed effort steadied him down.

He'd do no good like this. It was a new experience in his adult life. He'd been little more than a kid when the war began, but now he was thirty-something years old – couldn't recall his exact birthdate – but had faced a lot of danger in civilian life. Gone to meet it deliberately, because he knew his enemy and had tracked him down and got him in his sights.

Damn! That's what it was! That's what made him feel so powerless. He didn't yet have his enemy close enough to reach.

'Then the answer's simple, you fool! *Get him in your sights!*'

There *had* to be a way to do it.

And he'd better find it – fast.

The girl was barely conscious.

She hung across the horse like an old sack, held in place by one of the killer's hands pressing into the middle of her back. Occasionally that hand wandered on her cringing body and she had to fight the urge to throw up.

The world was passing in a red-grey haze – blurred, jumping about. She felt so groggy she had to close her eyes, but this somehow made the jolting, falling sensation worse.

Groping for a hold she grabbed his thigh by mistake and gave a small cry as she quickly withdrew her hand and almost slipped off.

'Hey! Don't be in such a hurry, sweetie. That felt good, your hand restin' there.'

She suddenly heaved up and back.

There was nothing conscious about the move: it was instinctive as her brain signalled her body a split second after she sorted out what it was telling her mind.

Her thrusting motion not only pushed his thigh away from the horse, it moved her body back, and she kicked wildly, breaking free of Brazos's casual grip. If he hadn't been so arrogant he might have roped her hands, or at least leaned some of his weight on her back to clamp her in position, but he figured she would stay put. *Wrong!*

She tumbled off the horse and the startled Brazos snatched wildly, but only at air. He quickly lunged down with his other hand, fingers locking into the material of her battered dress.

The fabric tore and she was suddenly airborne, but for only a very few seconds.

She cried out in alarm as the pounding hoofs of the racing horse flashed bare inches from her, and then her face stung as sand was flung up and she closed her eyes swiftly. A few grains got under the lids, and a few grains in the eye was all it needed to bring on temporary blindness, and a lot of pain as the grit scraped the eyeballs.

She hit hard, breath exploded from her lungs. Her body spun and bounced, completely disorienting her. There was a thump on the tip of her left shoulder from one of the horse's legs and she was flung clear while Brazos rocked wildly in the saddle, fighting the mount now as it weaved and snorted, annoyed by all the sudden, shifting weights.

Spitting sand, seeing the jarring world through a watery haze, tasting blood, Margaret somehow thrust up and— *What could she do now?*

The thought rammed into her mind as she swayed, knowing there was only one thing she could do: *run!*

And a lot of good that would do her! But she ran

135

anyway, stumbling, thrusting up through the cloying sand, startled – and pleased – to see Brazos had yanked so hard on the reins that he had pulled the horse off-balance and it was going down.

They were on a slope here and Brazos, looking around frantically for her while he tried to control the now-panicking horse, yanked the reins at the wrong moment.

Horse and rider fell outward, towards the lower slopes, Brazos skidding and spinning. The animal, sliding half on its back, whinnying in panic, rolled completely over Brazos, mashing him into the sand.

Margaret couldn't believe it: the horse was lying across the killer's lower legs, its weight driving him deeper into the hot, loose sand. The rest of him – the part that was free – clawed and flailed as he tried to yell, his hands like talons pulling more sand down towards him. It piled up under his chin and then his gasping mouth filled and he began to suffocate.

Halfway to her feet, bent almost double on the slope as she tried to find enough leverage to straighten up, Margaret Towney paused, watching Brazos in horror, as he made wrenching, hawking sounds that turned her stomach.

She staggered as she managed to get more or less upright, the horse rising from behind the pile of sand its body had pushed up during the slide down the slope. It stood there on quivering legs, shaking its head, sending clouds of sand flying as it pawed the ground, sneezing with a peculiar half-rasping, half-whistling sound that made her shudder.

But her gaze was drawn back to Brazos and the awful sounds he was making.

She turned her head quickly, didn't want to see the plum-coloured congestion deepening on his contorted face, the sand-coated protruding tongue, the eyes beginning to bulge—

And that did it!

Those damned eyes! They settled on her and – *surely she must be mistaken!* – they settled on her and *pleaded for help!*

Her mind was racing. She must be crazy! Crazy to read such a message in those terrible eyes. *Absolutely crazy* to even *consider* giving the smallest thought to complying!

Then he spat some sand, his body heaving as he tried to expel more from his drooling mouth.

'*H-elp meee. . . !*'

She knew she was noted around Hatfield for her fierce temper and a lot of folk claimed it was because she had been spoiled rotten by doting parents and got whatever she wanted by a series of deliberate tantrums. She could love strongly, and perhaps hate even more strongly, but she could not stand by and merely watch someone die, not even a depraved – *thing*, like Brazos McGraw. Not when she was close enough to help and fully capable of doing so . . . *dangerous though it would be.*

She could not kill someone in cold blood and that's what this would amount to if she didn't act humanely.

She had been sure she could have killed Mitchell

Slade with a shotgun that time for shooting her father, but, she had hesitated, begun a mental argument with herself and Slade's right to defend himself and it simply hadn't happened. Thank God!

But surely this was different! Brazos was no better than an animal, and – and—

She'd waited too long to act!

He caught her by one arm, twisting cruelly even as she tried to entice the horse to move away from his legs.

He spat a mouthful of wet sand into her face and she fell, repelled, clawing at it wildly and suddenly it was all over.

She might just as well have stayed flung across the saddle.

Even as the thought came, he threw her on her back, rammed a knee into her chest, pinning her down by her shoulders as he bared his stained teeth.

She was his prisoner once again.

The old field-glasses had a cracked lens and the poorly refined and cast glass had a yellowish tinge. The original clarity was long gone and Slade figured it was time he got rid of them. They had served him well, taken from the body of a Yankee officer he had killed in one of his first bayonet fights, and later presented to him by his colonel when he recovered from his wounds in the field hospital.

He'd even forgotten which battle it had happened in.

He looked at the glasses now, turning them this

way and that; the clarity they had once given was long past. He gritted his teeth, flung the glasses from him.

What he had been able to see was mostly blurred, but it was a hell of a lot clearer in his mind than it had been in the lenses.

In his mind, he had *been there*! Right alongside Margaret as she tried to avoid the touch – the clutch! – of Brazos. He felt his jaws clamp at the image and knew he would be unable to shake it for a long time.

But he could use it: use it to drive him on through blinding sandstorms, or cloudbursts, and forest fires if necessary. Overreacting, sure, but he needed that motivation.

He would catch up with Brazos McGraw; he only hoped that Margaret would still be with him – and alive – when he did. He didn't want to think beyond that.

Didn't *dare*!

Brazos aimed to play with him, lead him on, taunt him, Slade knew that. He *didn't* know just how well he could take it: bracing himself was one thing. Actually *being* taunted, mocked, or carefully led into some lightly disguised trap, well, *he* could fight his way out, all right, but what about Margaret?

She would be the bait and therefore the one to suffer most.

He knew Brazos well enough to figure that out.

Slade was tough: his nickname in the Marshals' Service was 'Hardcase' because of the many life-threatening situations he had been through and survived.

That was fine *for him*!

The first time there had been a crack in what he – and everyone who knew him – figured to be his 'armour' had been when the word came through that Angie had been kidnapped by his worst enemy: Brazos McGraw, of course.

His surprise at how he had reacted had turned into out-and-out shock when he found himself, for the first time he could remember, almost paralyzed, unable to call upon the always-ready action he had used during those years of danger.

It took no time at all to find the answer: because the victim, the person being used to tie his hands and put lead boots on his feet, was Angie, the woman he loved.

Worrying about her safety had kept him in shackles of torment, slowed him down, so that he started to lose confidence in his ability, something that had never happened before.

Now it was happening again!

'No!' he said aloud. 'Not this time! I have to stop Brazos and the only way is to kill him. I've got to find a way to do it so that Margaret survives.'

And once again he couldn't do a damn thing without a horse!

The answer came to him when he made himself sit down and clean the sand and grit from the actions of his Colt and Winchester. Just doing something that was positive eased some of the tension, allowed his sodden mind to explore possibilities even as he worked.

But the answer lay in Hatfield.

Swearing, he paused and looked around him, here at the edge of the desert – his quarry far out there, becoming smaller and more indistinct by the minute.

A horse had always been the answer, of course, but he had allowed his brain to tell him – *logically* – that he would lose ground and time by going back to Hatfield, or branching off to one of the scattered ranches.

But the answer *was* in Hatfield.

With McKendrick!

The man had even offered him horses enough to form a posse if he'd figured one was necessary, and—

He blinked, for a moment actually swaying with a wave of dizziness: a rider was coming down from the low range that stood between Hatfield and this part of the desert where it swung in close.

A rider, leading two mounts, one of which was saddled, waved frantically so as to catch his attention.

'By God, that *is* McKendrick!'

He simply stood there then until the man rode up, holding the bunched reins of the spare mounts.

McKendrick was sweating, looked a little wary.

'Figured you might be able to use these. Desert's a son of a bitch on foot.'

Slade was already swinging aboard the saddled mount, a big dun with a leery eye on him as he settled into leather. He noted the bulging set of saddle-bags and couldn't help the puzzled frown as he looked at McKendrick.

'How come, Mac?'

'You gimme a break with Red and that murderous little sidekick of his. 'Sides, I owe you for lettin' some bastard rig that shotgun set-up in the room I'd rented you.'

Slade smiled thinly, reached across and shook hands briefly.

'That scratches the itch I had between my shoulders, I guess. Just didn't realize what it was.'

McKendrick grunted, gestured to the fast disappearing dot of Brazos and Margaret.

'Wouldn't waste time, Marshal. Brazos knows the desert. He'll see you comin' but there ain't much you can do about that.'

'I've just got to hope that the sonuver won't harm Margaret until I get close enough to see – and hear. Then?' He shrugged, face very grim. 'In the lap of the gods, as they say, Mac.'

'Judas, Marshal! It-it's one helluva fix, ain't it?'

'That about describes it. *Gracias* again, Mac. Whatever happens, I won't forget this!'

He lifted a hand, swung the dun around, the reins tightening and bringing a snort from the second mount, a roan with a sleek hide that glistened in the brassy sun.

'Luck!' McKendrick called after him. 'Put a couple of bullets into that bastard for me!' He added more quietly, 'Might've had some grandkids if it hadn't been for him.'

He gazed out at the desert again now as the marshal rode out towards the first sandhill.

McKendrick felt the prick of hot tears, and brushed a hand quickly across his eyes, momentarily blurring the desert and the pulsing heat rising from it.

Somewhere out there – *somewhere* – was the body of his daughter, his only child. Only Brazos knew where. *No! That murdering bastard wouldn't even remember.*

'*Ride him down, Marshal!*' he yelled as Slade worked his way up and over the sandhill. 'Ride him down! Ride over an' over him till he's no more'n a. . . .'

He choked then and turned his mount back towards the town, shoulders shaking, head bowed.

CHAPTER 13

SLADE'S LAW

McKendrick had always had a reputation as a man who knew his horses, though it had taken him a long time before he bought the land and built his own ranch to run a string.

It was mixed stock, like most of the ranches in this part of the country, and he had gone back into the ranges, trapped the wild mustangs and broken them in, matched them at stud with three special-purchase mares and got himself a hardy breed that showed as much or more stamina in desert travel as other horses specially imported or trained for that particular chore.

His ranch being in the position it was – close to well-timbered hills, within spitting distance of the edge of the desert – and with more than a few men seeking out his help to get them away and out of the law's jurisdiction, McKendrick prospered.

144

But then he married and, already middle-aged, was looking forward to children, even grandchildren, to carry on his name. He had always had a special feeling towards women, not just his younger wife and their daughter, but women in general.

He nudged the law a little – all right: broke it in many ways, helping men on the run to get clear – for pay, of course. *But*, if any man who had been mixed up in the death or attack and injury of a woman came to him, that man paid his money – maybe more than the usual amount – and was given directions that inevitably ended in those men becoming lost in a part of the desert that was plumb *vicious* and would bake a man's hide off his bones.

He was proud to say that none survived.

McKendrick felt no remorse. Then Lucy, his daughter, disappeared, abducted by Brazos McGraw and his gang. When Marshal Mitchell Slade had finally captured that snake and put him behind bars, McKendrick mentally swore that if ever Slade needed help, he was the man to give it.

Slade had learned of McKendrick's attitude and side-line and, once, went to arrest him for helping men on the dodge escape the law, but when he realized that sometimes – quite a few *sometimes* – many of those men were given directions that only ended up with them dying in the desert, he came to regard McKendrick as more of a help than a hindrance.

And that was why he had no hesitation in following McKendrick's directions now.

They were precise and made a lot of sense.

'Might seem to most folk,' Mac had allowed, 'that Brazos is headin' for the State Line. Fact, I b'lieve you said he'd mentioned it? Uh-huh: plantin' the idea in your head . . . I mean he *could* be makin' for the Line, I can't be absolutely sure, but knowin' a little about the sneaky way that bloody-handed skunk operates, I reckon he's gonna swing north at Pilgrims' Crossing an' make a run away from the Line, take a chance and cross the flats they call Hell's Balcony – an' it *is* a slice of Hell itself. But, put it behind you, and you got all them Manzano Mountains to hide in. Water, greenery, game. Some day it might get developed into a fine place to settle, but for now, it's like one big damn' oasis, in the middle of a desert.'

Slade had heard of this place, never seen it, and, in fact, hadn't known it was so close to this area.

'Obliged, Mac. I never did think *you'd* had anything to do with the booby-trap in that room.'

'Well, I'm a man likes to get things all cleared away, you know what I mean? I still feel it shouldn'ta happened. So you go nail that Brazos an'. . . .' He shrugged.

'Mac, you're a man to ride the river with.'

McKendrick had snorted. 'More like a crick, these days.'

'You ain't that old.'

'Parts of me are. Why I ride with a cushion between me and the saddle.'

Slade tried hard not to smile.

'Reckon I need a few directions, Mac. Brazos has

one helluva start. I can't let him get too far ahead, not when he's got Margaret . . . and the way he thinks.'

McKendrick was all business now, took a battered tally book and a stub of pencil out of his shirt pocket.

'Draw you a map.' Mac looked up quickly. 'Or I could show you the way?'

'Reckon I'll travel faster alone, Mac.'

'Yeah, likely right. I'll sketch it in for you. . . .'

Slade had learned a long time ago that wearing a badge and administering the law called for more than just dotting the 'I's' and crossing the 'T's'. You had to give a little – how much, and in which direction, was entirely up to the badge-toter. And it could even be fatal if he guessed wrong or was outwitted. Then you had to live with your mistakes and try like hell not to make the same ones again.

So far, Marshal Mitchell Slade had been lucky.

Except for Angie. . . .

The desert heat was getting to Slade: he had been in hotter places, but he knew his tensions were making him edgy so he couldn't relax or think clearly.

There was that constant thought hammering in his head: *what if I foul up and Margaret is killed?*

By God! *That* would be hard to live with. *Mighty* hard. Fact was, he didn't think he'd want to go on living under those circumstances. Not two women in his life dying at the hands of the same damn maniac!

Be honest, Slade: her father would always stand

between you. Possibly there could be reconciliation, but only possibly. It had to be worth a try!

But that would come later: first he had to save her.

He squinted in the burning sunlight, lifted a hand and used it as well as the wide brim of his hat to shade his eyes.

And, suddenly, he felt as if a horse had kicked him in the midriff.

Brazos and Margaret were nowhere in sight.

While feeling sorry for himself, he'd lost them!

Margaret knew she wouldn't live through this.

She had already taken a bad beating. Maybe not so much in the sense that she had been battered with fists or some kind of weapon: she had, but she could live with bruises or a few scars – they would heal with time, *but – mentally?*

That was it: her brain couldn't absorb much more of the horror she'd already been through and the truth was she was sickeningly afraid of what *new* unpleasantness Brazos might think up. She knew it wouldn't be hard for him, not someone with his twisted brain.

She was afraid that she wouldn't be able to stand it. Life had been reasonably kind to her so far: she had had rough patches, like everyone else, probably no worse than anyone else, but it all came down to the individual and how they reacted – how *much* they reacted – sometimes overreacted: as she had when learning of her father's death at the hands of Mitchell Slade. It had been perhaps natural but, inevitably, humiliating, though still damn hard to take!

And the fact was still inescapable: Mitchell Slade had killed her father – in self-defence, maybe, but he had done it.

'Oh!' she said aloud. 'How can I be so interested in him knowing that?' She had no answer.

Just as she decided this, and began to compose herself for the worst, Brazos suddenly tipped her off the horse, violently, so that she gave a loud scream of shock. Her head whipped back and forth painfully, and then she was rolling in the fine, burning sand, half-choked, instinctively squirming and twisting away from the staggering horse's hoofs.

Staggering!

Yes! The poor animal had been lashed and spurred relentlessly – and needlessly, she thought – as they rode deeper into the desert. She lay there gasping, and then Brazos landed beside her, putting down one hand to steady himself before thrusting up to his feet.

He stumbled and the ailing mount crashed into him.

Its rump grazed his shoulder and the big head swung around and crashed into his face as he staggered.

Margaret couldn't believe it as blood splashed from his crushed nose and mouth and his whole body left the ground. He fell hard: it was on the slope, and his legs gave way so he started to roll and slide towards her.

Fear grabbed her like a grizzly's claw: she wanted to scream but was unable to as her throat closed. Brazos was obviously dazed and she saw, not without some pleasure, that one of his teeth had penetrated his lower lip. It looked mighty painful and she shuddered, but not with any sympathy for the killer, just at the ugliness of the wound.

He moaned and rolled his upper body, using his boots to slow his slide. Margaret looked around frantically and saw the horse struggling to regain its feet, the loose sand sliding out from under its scrabbling hoofs.

With a small cry she launched herself at the saddle, caught the horn just as the animal heaved up and she was yanked off her feet, slammed face first into the arched neck. She saw stars but didn't lose consciousness, and then her fingers twisted and locked in the mane.

She was slammed into the horse again, the animal beginning to really panic now, but she hooked an arm over the neck, tried to lift a foot into the jerking stirrup. It was too difficult. So she jumped, both arms going around the arched neck this time. She was dragged off her feet, face buried in the smelly, sweaty, sand-clogged hide, but she managed to get a leg across the saddle and the mount raced off, whinnying, in a mild panic.

With a final effort she heaved up into the saddle.

Startled at her success, she looked down at Brazos, who was just now gathering himself after the horse had knocked him down. One look at her and he snatched at his six-gun only to find the holster empty.

She even noticed his flash of panic as he realized he was without the weapon, stopped in his lunge for the horse and looked around frantically.

There it was! Half-buried in the sand. He grabbed at it, whirled as she urged the horse away, but somehow the animal had become confused and tried to *climb* the slope.

The sand was very loose here and it floundered, the girl flung about in her precarious perch in the saddle like a rodeo rider.

That was when Brazos, on his knees, lifted his gun.

The first two pulls on the trigger produced nothing but mild grating noises, sand getting into the works, he acknowledged bitterly and, still holding the Colt, he ran a few steps, then leapt up at the girl.

He wasn't high enough to get an arm about her neck but he clutched part of her already torn dress and it was enough to drag her back over the horse's rump. They went down in a tangle – horse, Margaret and Brazos. Arm flailing wildly he somehow squeezed the trigger again and this time the Colt fired.

It was almost beside the horse's ear and it shrilled, reared with its head thrashing. It just missed Margaret, but knocked her flat by ramming into her shoulder. Brazos tried to jump out of the way, started falling, and his gun fired again, his grip so loose that it jumped from his hand.

Margaret kicked away from the thrashing mount.

It dodged her riding boot, swinging its upper body – this time into Brazos as he rose out of the sand, wavering, on a collision course he couldn't avoid.

He catapulted back down the slope, hit at an awkward angle and lay there, blinking, face half buried, coughing.

The horse managed to struggle up and Margaret made a desperate lunge for the bridle, but she missed and the horse ran, plunging downslope this time.

Brazos was just getting upright when, dazed, he spun, hands coming up . . . and the horse hit him hard. Still frightened, the animal reared and pawed frantically.

Brazos McGraw made a gurgling sound as a hoof crashed into his ribs and the horse kicked him away like so much trash, his body rolling and skidding.

He lay there, gagging, holding his side through the ripped fabric of his shirt.

Margaret looked around frantically for a way to get out of there. But, mind all mixed up with the action, diving first this way, then the other, instead of running, she began to search for Brazos's dropped gun.

He lay there on his side now, grimacing, trying to hold a bunched section of his tattered shirt over his new wound.

'D-Don't s'pose you'd care to strap me up with my shirt, huh, swee'meat?' he gasped. 'Think I've busted a coupla . . . ribs. . . .'

Slowly she looked at him and her own battered

152

face straightened as she swallowed and slowly shook her head, momentarily stunned that he had the utter *gall* to ask for her help.

'Figures!' he groaned. 'S'pose I'll haveta m-make you!'

She froze as he lifted the six-gun he had pulled out of the sand and the barrel wavered not six inches from her face. She had plenty of dirt on it, smears of blood and recent bruises and swelling, but, under it all there was a sudden paleness as blood drained from her features.

She jumped, stomach muscles knotted, when he *laughed*!

'Dunno what to do, huh? Got your chance handed to you on a plate an' – an' you still dunno what to do!'

She was rigid now, eyes on the gun as it wavered around, but still covering her.

'Got your attention, have I? *Hah!* If you think I'm gonna waste a bullet on you ... make it nice an' quick. . . .' He was gasping for breath, pressing his free hand against his ribs. Then he shook his head slowly, side to side. 'Uh-*uh*! I'm feelin' kinda poorly, but a couple nice screams from you'll pick me up. . . .'

'No!' she gasped, putting her hands up in front of her face instinctively, terrified again.

'Ah, *yeah*! Not quite as I planned, but I can still enjoy things an' – an' make an interestin' package outa you for Slade to find.'

'You – you're *insane*!' she croaked.

153

He shrugged. 'Might be. But it ain't a bad feelin'. Damn ribs're sore, but hell, I've been hurt worse workin' on a cow with a runnin'-iron. You'll find out just how good . . . I-I'm feelin' . . . in a minute or two. . . .'

'*Not interested!*'

She shouted the words and saw with satisfaction that he started in surprise as she'd hoped he would.

Then she leaned down swiftly and scooped up a handful of sand and threw it towards him.

She had been aiming at his face but he was able to dodge and his desperate movement made him lose his footing. He cursed bitterly as he went down. The gun went off and she gave an involuntary cry, fell sprawling, slid a little way towards him, deliberately wrenched around to widen the distance just as he launched himself in her direction.

He grunted as he landed hard, fumbled the gun and gave it his attention so he could retrieve it.

On all fours now, Margaret scrabbled and dug her hands deep in the sand as she tried to get to her feet. She knew that going uphill was dangerous, but she couldn't risk sliding any closer to him as, snarling now, blood from the tooth-wound in his lip spreading across his contorted face, he lunged towards her again.

She kicked sand towards him, didn't wait to see if it had reached him, twisted and continued her climb.

The sand was too loose!

She could not get purchase: her hands dug in almost to the wrists, but the sand came away almost

154

as if it was liquid; she lost more distance than she gained with each clawing effort.

She was sliding back towards him!

His laugh chilled her blood.

He watched her lose ground, her struggles turning her so she fell on her side. But she twisted frantically, trying to dig her heels in, hands groping now to act as brakes.

He shook his head from side to side, grinning through his blood mask, rose halfway and spread his arms.

'Come to Poppa, sweetmeat! Got somethin' for you an'—'

The taunting stopped abruptly.

His blood ran cold as he saw her looking past him, slightly downslope. He gave an involuntary yell and scrambled awkwardly to his feet, wincing and swaying as sudden pain in his side caught him, even as he stared at Marshal Mitchell Slade standing, four-square, at the foot of the slope, Colt in hand.

The girl was stunned at first, then cried one word, full of relief: '*Mitch!*'

'You hurt bad?' he asked, without taking his eyes off Brazos.

'I'll manage. Oh, Mitch, how did you get here?'

'Lost sight of you, but then there were a couple of gunshots from over this way and here I am.' His gun barrel jerked. 'On your feet, Brazos.'

But the killer merely smiled crookedly with his bloody mouth and sat down, drawing up his knees and resting his forearms on them.

'Reckon I'm too tired.'

'You want to die lying down? OK, guess it'll save a little time. Can just roll you into the grave.'

Brazos laughed again, more a sneer this time. 'Who the hell you tryin' to kid? You ain't gonna shoot me! Beat-up like I am, an' after what I've done to your gal.' He shook his head. 'Nosir! Ain't your style! Oh, you might kill me eventually but—'

While talking fast as a diversion, he brought up his gun in a blur and there was a dull *click*! as he pulled the trigger: it was either clogged again with sand or the cartridge was fouled.

Brazos looked savage for a moment, then snarled – although it may have been meant as some kind of disdainful smile.

'Dammit! An' damn your goddamn luck, Slade!'

He threw the Colt at the marshal, who was ready for such a move and ducked as the gun crashed into brush lining the sandy slope.

But while he had been ready to dodge the thrown Colt, Slade was not ready for Brazos hurling himself across the short distance.

Margaret screamed and Slade dropped, slipped on the incline and slid down a few feet. Brazos kept coming, grunting with the effort to increase his speed, and then he threw himself bodily at Slade again.

Arms spread, he crashed into the lawman and locked his hands around his throat. The girl screamed, but she had fallen and was also busy trying to stop sliding down the incline, loose sand following her.

Slade drove a fist into Brazos's body and the man moaned sickly, half-doubled over, then heaved forward, driving his head into Slade's midriff. The marshal gagged and one leg folded under. Brazos got his boots set and drove his head into the lawman's body again. Slade lifted a knee savagely and caught Brazos on the side of the head as he tried to throw himself back.

His legs tangled and he went halfway down, one hand clawing into the ground and supporting his weight. He simply spun on it like a fulcrum, a leg extended, and Slade stumbled just as he swung a kick at Brazos's head.

The killer dropped flat, rose again immediately and the lawman cannoned into him with his own forward movement. Brazos grabbed for his throat again and this time he managed to put pressure on the windpipe. Slade automatically reached for the hands, trying to prise the crushing fingers away. He got two free, bent one back until Brazos yelled in pain as it was about to snap. The killer managed to get it free but he turned away, holding the damaged hand against his chest.

Almost unhurriedly, Mitchell Slade stepped after him, straight-armed him a blow on the mouth that snapped Brazos's head back. Mitch felt the protruding tooth break off and Brazos howled, spat blood and spittle at Slade's face.

The lawman weaved aside, half-turning as he wiped his face and spun back instantly, catching Brazos as the man rushed in, thinking he could

157

batter Slade from behind.

Instead, Slade's arms blurred as he hammered his fists like pistons into Brazos's ribcage and a couple into his face. The man back-pedalled frantically, putting his hands up in front of his face now, leaving his midriff unprotected again.

Slade took advantage of the opening and hammered at the man's ribs. Brazos grunted, not just once but in a series of a half-dozen grating gasps, clawed hands groping for a grip on the lawman, hanging on awkwardly as he wavered, trying to stay upright. The marshal kicked his legs out from under him and when he fell, drove two hard boots into the man's back. Brazos screamed, freezing the girl in shock, and then he rolled, sliding down the slope, legs kicking until he crashed into the base of a berry-loaded bush and his head rapped the trunk.

He lay there, dazed, while Slade stood, half-bent, drawing in long, gulping breaths. Margaret, concerned, ran to him, tripping once, then took him by the left arm.

'You— Are you all right?' she gasped.

He nodded, held her tighter than he meant to and worked his mouth until his words became intelligible as he asked if she, too, was all right.

'Yes! Yes, I believe I am!' she answered, sounding somewhat surprised. Then she threw her arms about Slade and hugged him tightly. 'Oh, Mitch! Mitch! I-I'm just so relieved! He-he explained to me what he was going to do next and—'

'*Next?* Slade snapped, looking into her eyes. What

I AM THE LAW!

... what did he do to you? *No!* You don't have to tell me, but—'

'It-it was awful!' She was shuddering now and he tightened his grip about her, holding his gun awkwardly and making sure the barrel was turned away in case he inadvertently pulled the trigger.

'It's all right now, Margaret. He's finished. When he gets back to Comstock this time he'll have years of solitary confinement – maybe right up until the day he dies. . . .'

He felt her shudder.

Then both of them tensed as Brazos's crazy laugh sounded.

He was crouched on all fours, blood-streaked, that mad look on his face.

'I'll get out again, Slade! You know damn well I will! Ain't no prison gonna hold me! Not with Miss Sweetmeat still alive an' smelling so nice an' just *waitin'* for . . . well, you know!' He paused and glared murderously at Mitch Slade. Then, shifting his gaze to the girl, pursed his lips and made kissing sounds that sent goosebumps running up and down her spine.

Her grip tightened painfully on Slade's left arm, and he felt the fear in her as she began to tremble. 'Oh, God!'

Short as it was, he knew it was a prayer . . . and glancing at her injuries he figured there were greater ones that he could not see, inside where they could grow and. . . .

But bars and brick walls topped with broken glass

would give her reassurance. *Or would they?*

Maybe she would always live with the fear that today or next week, even next year would be the one when Brazos McGraw would make good his boast that no prison could hold him.

Brazos laughed again. 'Just look at her, Slade! How about we do a deal? Lemme go and I'll scoot up to Canada and you'll never hear from me again. Huh? How about it? Be a better deal than you puttin' me back in the Pen. Come on! You ain't gonna take me back to that hell-hole, Mitch! You know you ain't!'

Mitch felt the girl's fingers tighten on his arm, her slim body pressing against him. He thought she was holding her breath.

He remained silent and Brazos stirred irritably.

'Come *on*! You've thought it over long enough. Do a deal! I've got more loot stashed. It's yours! Take it all! It'll leave me nothin', *but*, I ain't goin' back inside!'

A moment's pause and then Slade nodded slowly.

'You're right, Brazos, you're not,' he said, and – as Brazos grinned – squeezed the Colt's trigger.